KNIGHT AND DAY

BRENDA BARRETT

"Wow," Pearl didn't answer. She was looking at him with her mouth half-opened. "You are one good-looking gardener."

Phillip smiled. "Thank you."

"If you were my gardener, I would get nothing done," Pearl said wonderingly.

Phillip smiled. "If you were my boss, I probably wouldn't get anything done either."

His eyes swept over her figure and then back up to her face, but this time she was snarling.

"You probably have a gazillion girlfriends, don't you? And a million and one children who you don't look after."

Madge groaned beside her. "Pearl..."

"Pardon me?" Phillip stuttered. She had gone from complimentary to accusatory in less than a second.

"Don't act like you don't know what I am talking about," Pearl put her hand akimbo. "I know your type."

"And what is my type?" Phillip gritted out.

"Good-looking, didn't do so well in school, had all the girls running you down, eating you out, that's why you are just a gardener. You probably don't even take care of your children."

ABOUT THE AUTHOR

Brenda Barrett is an award-winning and bestselling author who has a passion for writing real Jamaican romances.

When she's not weaving words that transport readers to exotic locales, you can find her nurturing her green thumb in the garden or doting on her beloved cats.

With an infectious zest for life, this author brings a unique perspective to her writing that is both relatable and thought-provoking.

Don't be surprised if you find yourself lost in the pages of her latest work, as she seamlessly blends romance with some drama, mystery, and suspense, or even sci-fi, leaving readers wanting more.

You can connect with Brenda online at:
Brenalbar.com
Twitter.com/AuthorWriterBB
Facebook.com/AuthorBrendaBarrett

Chapter One

Phillip needed to think, and he needed to do it away from Chex's party. His brother was throwing a bash by the poolside, and the music was so loud that he could feel the reverberations in the house.

He could faintly hear the party from here, the sound wasn't as intrusive as it was closer to the house. He considered this part of the Hastings estate as his own personal oasis. It was the perfect place to ruminate and air out his brain. He was in no frame of mind to join Chex's friends and party. They were not his crowd or his type of people.

He had declined the invite and had escaped to his garden. It was here that he had rediscovered his love for gardening.

There was something about tending to and cultivating plants that centered him. His favorite plants were roses, and he had gone a little giddy and bought dozens of different varieties and different colors. He planted them himself and tended to them when he had the time. When he didn't have time, he asked the main gardener to help.

He had completely taken over the abandoned space. In his grandfather's day, it had been a playground for his mother, but since his mother had grown up, it had been abandoned as a play area and the gardeners had just used it as a lawn.

Phillip had totally transformed the area. He had fenced it with cute picket fences and created two entrances where he had planted pink climbing roses on arched trellises. He had also placed two of the most fragrant climbing roses under the trellis at each end of the garden.

He always came out here in his rattiest outfit with his gardening tools, ready to work on his rose bushes, especially when he was wrestling with something on his mind. He headed for the east side of the garden with his sheers.

His relationship with Helena loomed large in his thoughts. It was at the forefront of his mind. He was forty years old and itching for something more permanent with her, but Helena, who was a year younger, had no such desires.

"How would that work, Phillip?" Helena asked when he brought it up. They were lying in bed after a lovemaking session that had not had the same intensity as it usually did. They saw each other infrequently, so they were usually hungry for each other, but not that day. That day, his mind was troubled.

"You are the head of the Hastings Group of Companies based in Jamaica, and I run my own practice here in Turks and Caicos. You wouldn't give up your company to come live with me, would you?" Helena looked at him incredulously.

"No," Phillip said.

"And I will not give up my practice or clients to live with you in Jamaica. I love it here," Helena said. "I like our arrangement. We visit each other when we can and enjoy our time together. Why change that?"

"Because we are both barreling toward fifty, with no plans to have a family or a more permanent arrangement," Phillip answered.

"I don't want to get married again, Phillip," Helena looked him in the eye seriously. "I thought you knew I wasn't joking when I said that six years ago. I am a happy divorcee. I don't want kids. I want to live my life free and unencumbered. Maybe we should reassess our arrangement if you are unhappy."

"Yes," Phillip nodded. "Maybe we should."

That was three weeks ago. He didn't know why he had upset the applecart; he was comfortable with Helena, they shared similar world views.

It must be something about him reaching the age of forty that had him reassessing his priorities.

Or was it that he was going through a midlife crisis? Or it could be that his father's recent stroke had affected him more than he thought.

Maurice Knight had never been the best father growing up. Phillip had escaped him and the farm he grew up on as soon as he could. He hadn't seen or spoken to the man in twenty-one years, but something about facing his father's mortality had shaken him up.

It had him reassessing priorities, questioning his legacy and what he would leave behind.

His father was awful when he was growing up, but at least he had sons, three of them. They carried his genetic material into the future, even if they didn't have his last name. Both he and his brother Chex had changed their name from Knight to Hastings, the surname of their mother's father. Their youngest brother Jack had kept the Knight. At least Maurice's surname would be carried into the future.

Did he want that? Did he want a legacy? A child or

children to keep the Knight/Hastings legacy burning bright? Was that what this was all about?

Was this insidious feeling enough to give up what he had with Helena? And if not Helena, who would he find as compatible?

She had come the closest to making him feel content in his forty years. They had been together for eight years all together. Two years when they were in law school and six years when they had reconnected after attending the same function.

It had taken one look across the room for them to know that their youthful relationship still had some legs. Helena had been freshly divorced; he had not had a long-term relationship since his time with her. The timing was perfect, but what now? What was he going to do?

He was snipping along an unruly climbing rose bush when he heard voices.

"Listen, Madge," a very attractive woman with an hourglass figure and a pretty face was saying. "I am not interested in Chex. He's handsome, he's rich, and you know that is a requirement if I am going to be taking up with any man, but he is not interested in anything long-term. I am not in the market for a short fling."

"I hear you, Pearl," Madge said.

"Ooh, it's nice in here," Pearl said. "Really pretty. I could stay in here all day long."

"There's the gardener," Madge whispered loud enough for Phillip to hear.

He turned around. "Ladies, good evening. You have wandered far away from Chex's party, haven't you? Unfortunately, visitors are not allowed around here. I will have to ask you to leave."

"Wow," Pearl didn't answer. She was looking at him

with her mouth half-opened. "You are one good-looking gardener."

Phillip smiled. "Thank you."

"If you were my gardener, I would get nothing done," Pearl said wonderingly.

Phillip smiled. "If you were my boss, I probably wouldn't get anything done either."

His eyes swept over her figure and then back up to her face, but this time she was snarling.

"You probably have a gazillion girlfriends, don't you? And a million and one children who you don't look after."

Madge groaned beside her. "Pearl..."

"Pardon me?" Phillip stuttered. She had gone from complimentary to accusatory in less than a second.

"Don't act like you don't know what I am talking about," Pearl put her hand akimbo. "I know your type."

"And what is my type?" Phillip gritted out.

"Good-looking, didn't do so well in school, had all the girls running you down, eating you out, that's why you are just a gardener. You probably don't even take care of your children."

Phillip took a step back. "Are you a friend of Chex?"

"Yes," Pearl said.

"Are you in the habit of making assumptions about people?" Phillip frowned. "You have no idea who I am."

"Oh really?" Pearl raised an eyebrow skeptically. "Then who are you?"

"I'm a hard-working man trying to make a living," Phillip answered. "I don't have any children. If I did, I would take care of them."

"Good answer," Pearl snorted. "Whether it's true or not is left to be seen."

"And you'll never know," Madge pulled Pearl towards

the entrance. "Sorry, mister, my friend is having a bad day. She's anti-man at the moment, and she decided to take it out on you."

Phillip watched them as they walked out of the garden, his eyes narrowed.

Pearl, he liked the name. He liked her figure. She made him forget what he was thinking about. It's a shame that she was crazy.

Chapter Two

"**W**ho is Pearl?" Phillip had asked his brother the day after his encounter with Pearl. That meeting had stuck in his head. When his eyes had met hers, there had been a moment of sudden clarity, almost like an otherworldly revelation that she would be significant in his life. He couldn't wait until he saw Chex to quiz him about her.

And for Chex, that was late in the evening when he was heading to the studio. Phillip had just got in from work and was having dinner.

As a music producer and party promoter, Chex's day started in the evenings. Phillip sometimes marveled at how Chex could keep up his lifestyle at his age. He partied every night without fail.

Most of the parties were business-related and networking opportunities, but Phillip suspected that many weren't. Chex just liked to party, and he attracted that kind of crowd to him. He wouldn't be surprised if Pearl was one of his party friends. He had never in all the time he lived with his brother been attracted to one of his party friends. In fact, he usually found them abhorrent in some way. This was a first for him.

He wondered how old Pearl was.

Chex was looking at him with a knowing grin on his face. "Pearl is not Helena."

"I know that," Phillip frowned. "Yesterday she came into my rose garden with her friend, Madge, and told me I was hot and that she wouldn't get any work done with me around. And when I returned the compliment, it's as if she switched, started snarling at me, and accusing me of, amongst other things, not taking care of my children."

Chex laughed. "That sounds like Pearl."

"Are you two lovers?" Phillip asked.

"No," Chex shook his head, "not for the lack of trying on my part, but Pearl has certain requirements that a man has to fulfill. I guess I don't qualify."

"What are the requirements?" Phillip asked.

"Well," Chex grinned, "you have to be rich."

Phillip nodded. "You are... and?"

"You have to be committed, responsible, and spontaneous," Chex continued. "And you have to be able to take her on adventures and keep her on her toes. And most of all, you have to make her feel loved and appreciated every day. She must be the center of your universe. I cannot offer any woman that right now, if ever. That sounds too much like marriage and commitment and mental stability, you know I get a bit crazy sometimes."

Phillip nodded. "So you told her all about that and she friend-zoned you?"

"Yup," Chex nodded. "I don't mind. She's a good friend. A genuinely nice person. She doesn't play games, and she's honest to a fault. What you see is what you get. If she is thinking about you, more than likely, she will tell you. She has a no-holds-barred approach to life. I like that in a person, male or female. So that's why she is my friend. All my male friends want to get with her because she's hot."

"That she is," Phillip murmured. "Quite shapely, perfect proportions."

"And has a face to go with it," Chex chuckled. "It makes you wonder how she could fend off so many men at Sensuous City, where she used to work. Madge said the men left her alone."

"Sensuous City?" Phillip asked. "It sounds like one of those ghastly places you love to frequent."

"It is," Chex grinned. "There are some good clean girls there who would be up for anything. Madge was one of them. I can't believe that you haven't heard that the famous DJ Duke got married to an exotic dancer. Madge is the girl. They met at Sensuous City when we were shooting a music video."

"I don't even know who DJ Duke is," Phillip frowned.

Chex sighed. "Of course, you wouldn't. You have zero interest in modern music."

"Are you saying that Pearl is a dancer at Sensuous City?" Phillip asked.

"Nope. She used to run the place," Chex grinned.

"She did?" Phillip asked. "How old is she?"

"Thirty-six," Chex got up and stretched.

"She doesn't look it," Phillip murmured.

"I know," Chex said. "She has a daughter who is twenty-one and married."

"Is that so?" Phillip asked, genuinely taken aback. He would have guessed Pearl to be in her late twenties, not thirties, and definitely not having a twenty-one year old daughter.

"That's one of the things that made me back away from her," Chex said. "She wants kids. She says she wants to enjoy motherhood this time around in a committed relationship with a man that she doesn't have to take to court for child support. I do not want kids. I vowed never to have any after my childhood."

"I know," Phillip said. "I thought the same, but I am rethinking that."

"I am not, that's non-negotiable, no kids ever." Chex said. "As a matter of fact, I am going to get a vasectomy done soon and even after that my partner has to be protected and so will I."

"That's quite drastic," Phillip said. "Why don't you wait a bit? Maybe you'll change your mind when you are forty like me. If I had gotten the snip earlier, I would have regretted it now."

"Nope," Chex shook his head. "Never going to change. I don't want Maurice Knight's genetic material to live on through me. You and Jack can handle that."

Phillip grunted.

What could he say? He had felt the same for years. Their father had started a cult in the hills of Trelawny when he was a baby and had treated all three of his sons appallingly. Punishment and bullying were how he had tried to keep them in line to prevent them from leaving.

Phillip had borne the brunt of it as the older of the three boys, but there had been less opportunity to punish him. He had been more pliable, and he hadn't rebelled. Instead, he had bided his time until he could leave.

Chex, on the other hand, had been rebellious from birth and had endured gross child abuse in the form of so-called discipline to get him to comply. He had been tied to the rafters on a crudely made cross to contemplate his sins more often than Phillip could count.

Their father had tried to break his spirit by locking him away without food or water in a dark space he called the Punishment House. Chex could not be broken though and had refused to play the game; it was as if he had wanted Maurice to kill him.

Phillip knew Chex still had nightmares about that time. It was no wonder that he opted not to sleep at night. The dark carried with it certain unspoken terrors. It had been the same for him at first, but he had long since sought therapy for his issues.

He could contemplate that time in his life without much bitterness. He could even go back to Knightsbridge Farm without having a full-on panic attack. In fact, he had returned for his youngest brother's wedding. He had even visited his father a time or two, who was rendered immobile by a stroke.

The first time visiting his father had jolted him. He had forgotten that he looked so much like him. Maurice Knight was an exact older copy of him, it's as if his mother Laurel Hastings Knight had not imparted any of her genetic material into his genetic makeup.

He could see his features in the man, and then the thought had come to him. Wouldn't it be nice to have a son who would look like him too?

He knew he would do a better job at fatherhood than his father had done. So why not try?

But who would he try with? Helena was not interested, which reminded him that he had to break it off with her.

He wanted a clean slate moving forward, unencumbered by any relationships.

His next relationship he would immerse himself into. He would be in it wholeheartedly, no long distance, no half effort. He wanted it to work forever. Maybe he would try being the sort of man that Pearl had outlined in her requirements to Chex.

And maybe he could be that man to Pearl.

No, not Pearl, she wasn't his type.

He was looking for a Helena type - a woman who had her own thing going on, probably a lawyer, one who loved debating the finer points of the law with him. Though he wasn't practicing, he had loved when Helena used him as a sounding board for her cases.

He wanted a woman who was considerate and caring and who would challenge him intellectually. Someone who could hold her own in any conversation, but also knew when to be a good listener.

He admired Helena for her strong character and independence, and he hoped to find someone who embodied those same qualities but finding the perfect woman was easier said than done.

Many of the women he met were either too focused on their careers to have a personal life or too dependent on him for their own happiness. Finding the perfect balance was going to be a near-impossible task.

"Before I forget," Chex interrupted his thoughts, "I have a buddy who is selling his luxury villas in St. Ann. He wants a quick, fast sale. It's a good investment. It's always booked, with some loyal repeat customers. And he just did some renovations."

Phillip raised an eyebrow. "Oh really? Why is he selling out?"

"He is moving back home to Spain, his father died, and the family business needs him."

"Oh," Phillip nodded. "I see."

"The property has three villas and an outdoor restaurant

that he rents for events. The location is perfect. It has an unencumbered view of the sea and has beach access. You can throw two parties simultaneously on the property, and it's always booked for events. Most of the operations, like booking and reservations, are automated.

"I am thinking of buying it, but he wants it sold like yesterday, and the price is steep. I don't want to put up so much money by myself. I need a partner."

"Send me the details, and I'll check it out," Phillip said. "If it looks good, I'll join you."

"Good, thanks, bro." Chex got up. "I am going all the way to Negril this evening. DJ Duke is the headliner for a concert there. So, a couple of us will stay at a villa and chill for some days. Pearl should be coming; I might tell her you asked about her."

"Please don't," Phillip grimaced. "My attraction to her was unexpected and will soon wear away. She's not my type."

****

"**I** can't believe I am seeing the day," Madge snickered, "when Pearl, my friend Pearl who hates men by default, is so bothered by a man that she is restless with it."

Pearl glared at her friend. "I am restless because I need a job, and I am concerned about what Leonard will do. I know he is out there just waiting to punish me for leaving Sensuous City."

"And not just any man," Madge ignored her, "oh no, this one is a gardener."

Madge laughed and held her side. "Pearl whose motto is 'if you are poor, I'll show you the door,' that Pearl."

"You are so immature," Pearl threw a sofa pillow at

Madge. "All I asked was who was he?"

"Over and over again," Madge said, "and you may have mentioned that he's got the most striking features you've ever seen, straight and narrow face, high cheekbones, and skin the shade of mocha. He's not too thin, with just the right muscular definition. A fine, fine man."

Pearl grunted. "I didn't say two fines, and I didn't say anything about the right muscular definition. You added that. I am so sorry; I snapped at him for no reason. I must be losing my mind."

"You'll get over it," Madge chuckled.

"I am trying," Pearl grunted. She flopped back in the settee and looked out at the patio with the spectacular views of the Negril coastline, a sense of discontent sweeping over her. What she needed was a job. If she had been working and busy, she wouldn't still be thinking and talking about this man. It's as if when their eyes had collided, she had been infected with a virus.

Pearl looked down at her nails. Since she had escaped from Leonard, she had gotten them done every week. She was living like a pampered queen and didn't like it.

She didn't know how people lived this kind of lifestyle for long. She had been staying with Madge and her husband, Duke for four months, and already she was bored out of her mind.

Duke was constantly booked and busy, and Madge traveled with him to concerts and events, which meant she was constantly traveling too. Duke usually moved about with an entourage; it was nothing to add one more to the list of hangers-on.

She was a part of his entourage now, it would seem. Her job, if you could call it that, was Madge's camerawoman.

Madge kept herself busy by recording her days on social

media. She shared what she ate for the week and where she went. Surprisingly, she got a lot of endorsements from that and was actually paid huge sums of money to be herself while endorsing products. Part of her notoriety came from her status as the wife of DJ Duke, but a big part of it was Madge herself. She was good at sharing her life, and people found her relatable.

Pearl could never do that. She had to be careful not to appear in Madge's videos or pictures. She didn't want Leonard to track her down.

Leonard Crooks. The man whose employ she had left, who refused to let her go. He became her stepbrother when her mother had married his father when they were both older people with adult children.

He was once her lover. A point in time, she didn't care to relish. It had felt more like an obligation rather than any true desire on her part. She had had her daughter, Jewel, at the time and was living with Pastor Brewster and his wife in the cottage behind their house when Leonard had come to her with the proposition: "I'll build you a place, you live there, I'll pay your bills, and in exchange, you become my woman."

Pearl hated thinking about that point in her life without a heaping serving of self-loathing. The only silver lining in that cloud was that she didn't have to be his woman that often. He had too many women in that role for her to be the center of attention, and she had liked it like that.

Her arrangement with Leonard had chipped away at her self-esteem, not that there was much left of it after her mother kicked her out of the house when she had gotten pregnant for Darnell Webb, her high school boyfriend. Darnell had allowed his jealousy of his brother to overshadow him during her pregnancy.

"You have a scowl on your face," Chex said, interrupting her thoughts.

Pearl laughed. "That seems to happen when I think about my exes."

"Ah," Chex grinned.

"At least that's a change of topic," Madge said. "Pearl here has been obsessing over your gardener."

"My gardener?" Chex asked.

"Yep, the one with the chiseled cheekbones and the handsome face. He could be a model or a movie star. He's probably in his mid to late thirties and quite fine. How did you get a gardener like that? What's his life story? Was he a model at some point? Some woman's toy boy?" Madge asked.

"I don't know who you are talking about," Chex muttered.

"Tall, medium brown complexion, a swimmer's body, well-honed and muscular but not too muscular," Pearl chimed in.

"You mean Phil?" Chex laughed. "Oh my!"

"His name is Phil?" Pearl prompted.

Chex looked like he would say more but thought better about it.

"Yep," Chex said, "but he is not..."

"Come on, guys," Duke interrupted them. "The food is ready. I am starving. I have to perform tonight, and I am going high octane. I need to eat."

He is what? Pearl wanted to ask when Chex looked at Duke and joked about something else. Maybe he was going to say not available or not single.

What did it matter? He was not rich and therefore did not meet the requirements she had for her future mate. She was not going to compromise about that one. She sighed. She could forget Phil. She would forget Phil.

Chapter Three

Philip stared in disbelief at the report Chex's secretary sent over. He requested a quarterly update on their joint investment, El Cielo, the luxury villas he had purchased with Chex. And though he had indicated to Chex that he would be a silent partner, he was not a hands-off partner. He wanted to know exactly what was going on in any of his business interests at all times.

That's just the way he was. And Chex knew that, and that was why he got a state of affairs report every quarter. Phillip had understood that they would keep the staff and change nothing.

So why was he staring at the sentence that said— new manager, Pearl Day.

Of all the people in the world, why would Chex hire Pearl Day to run a set of luxurious villas?

It was a profitable concern, and that was why Phillip had made the investment.

Chex should have recruited someone with experience in managing villas. Not a friend, who by his brief encounter with her, had made assumptions about him and snarled at him?

Phillip got up from his desk and started pacing. What was he going to do about this? And why did he have such a visceral reaction to seeing the woman's name?

His encounter with Pearl had been brief. It should have been a blip in his otherwise busy life, but she persisted in his memory with sharp clarity. He could probably paint her features by now; if he had the skills to draw. He would lovingly outline her perfectly arched brows, high cheekbones, cute, upturned nose, and eyes the color of coffee surrounded by thick eyelashes that surely couldn't be real.

He sat down and read over the rest of the report, trying to push Pearl from his mind.

Repairs need to be done on the gazebo on the west lawn, and a flower garden, fountain, or something of interest would be perfect there, as recommended by new manager Pearl Day.

Goodness, her name again.

Phillip brought up the file named El Cielo on his laptop and looked at the detailed video. He had the real estate person record the video for his perusal when he was considering purchasing the property with Chex because he hadn't been able to make it to the place in person.

He fast-forwarded to the clips of the gazebo. It indeed needed repairs, and it would benefit from some décor, not that the backdrop wasn't good enough, but he could see why she would recommend a flower garden.

He could picture it with white roses, their white petals would be in the foreground with the sea in the distance.

In his mind's eye, he could see a variety of roses on the

west lawn, with climbers taking over half of the gazebo and ramblers along the fence. If some accent lights were added, that area would be a fragrant moon garden at night.

He could imagine the fragrance of the plants and how impressive it would all be.

He dragged his mind away from that fantasy and glanced at the clock. It was one thirty, time to berate his brother for making Pearl Day manager of their latest acquisition.

Why was he so angry about it, though?

Maybe because that brief encounter with Pearl had not left his mind. He still thought about her in the three months since he had seen her in his garden and the fact that she was still a feature in his thoughts was a mystery to him.

She had a pretty face, but pretty faces were a dime a dozen in his world. He steepled his fingers under his chin.

What he felt for her was an instant relentless attraction. He hadn't felt that way in years, even with Helena.

He must be lonelier than he thought since the breakup.

He hadn't managed to replace her yet, but that was to be expected. He was working around the clock. The Hastings group of companies had branched out into other businesses besides the core hardware stores. He had been obligated to closely watch some of them to see if they were worth the investment.

He picked up the phone to call Chex and was just about to hang up after several rings when Chex answered.

"What's up, bro?" Chex asked, his voice still sounding sleepy.

"You hired Pearl Day," Phillips said. "Without consulting me."

Chex chuckled. "I had to do it on the quiet because I know you would say no."

"How do you know I would say no?" Philip asked.

"Because I know you," Chex said. "You would call one of those recruitment agencies and probably find someone who was managing villas for a hundred years and could do this in their sleep."

"That's right!" Phillip yelled. "That's what business people do!"

"I run a business," Chex said, "a very profitable one. Don't tell me about what business people do."

Phillip had no comeback for that. Chex had somehow managed to marry his partying habits with his ear for music into a thriving business. He was even producing mainstream productions and doing exceptionally well at it.

"I'm sorry," Phillip said grudgingly. "I meant conventional business people. We don't just point to a groupie and say— you, run my business. You look pretty enough."

"Pearl is not a groupie," Chex grunted. "She was bored. She's going out of her mind, and she has a good mind. Why waste it?"

"Is that so? I thought she was having a whale of a time hanging out on yachts with Madge, going to high-end restaurants, and being a general groupie."

"How would you know that?" Chex asked.

"Madge refers to her as PD, her bestie for life," Phillip said, and then realized that he was revealing too much.

Chex laughed. "So you have taken to stalking Madge?"

"No, I wouldn't call it stalking. My secretary is a fan of her videos. I may have mentioned that she is a friend of yours and she may be keeping me up to date on Madge and her friend PD, unsolicited of course. PD never shows her face on camera but always cracks Madge up," Phillip cleared his throat. "Anyway, the point of this call is to say that because she is your friend does not mean she is good enough to manage three luxurious villas."

"She has the experience," Chex said. "She managed Sensuous City for years; that's a major nightclub. The guesthouse will be a walk in the park for her. Besides, she's been there a month now, and there are no complaints."

"Is that so?" Philip asked. "I'm going to have to find out for myself."

"What do you mean?" Chex said. "Please don't create any ruckus, Philip. It's already done. She's hired. She signed an employment contract. I am not in the habit of signing and breaking contracts for no reason."

"I'm not creating a ruckus," Philip said. "I'm just going to check up on my investment."

"She thinks you're the gardener," Chex chuckled. "She asked me about you too, you know."

"Is that so?" Philip asked, suddenly intrigued.

"I had a hard time working out who she was talking about until she described how handsome you were," Chex said. "I think she mentioned something about chiseled cheekbones. I didn't tell her that you were my brother."

"Oh," Phillip leaned back in his chair, an idea was forming in his head. A diabolical one. "You didn't tell her I am your brother, so she still thinks I am the gardener?"

"That's right," Chex chuckled. "You said she wasn't your type, so I left it alone."

"What are you doing with the west lawn?" Phillip asked. "She suggested flowers or a fountain or something like that. I agree with her."

"Ah," Chex said, "I was thinking about fixing the gazebo and having her hire a landscaper."

"I was thinking that it would look good with white roses around that area. Maybe some curling around the gazebo and a few arches on entering the area, with the sea as a backdrop. It would look gorgeous. If done right, it would probably be the most visited part of the property."

"That sounds nice," Chex said, unimpressed.

"If only you could picture it," Phillip was irked by his lack of interest. Chex was a creature of the night, not interested in flowers or anything remotely garden related.

"If you say so," Chex said. "Maybe you could tell the landscaper that. I am indifferent."

"My vacation is coming up," Philip said. "I was thinking of taking my full two months this year. I had plans to Europe hop with Helena, but now there is no Helena…."

"You are not asking me to Europe hop with you, are you?" Chex asked, aghast.

"No," Phillip laughed, "you and I have different interests. While I would go to museums, immerse myself in history, and be inclined to more daytime entertainment, you would only be interested in the nightlife. By day two, you would have many questionable-looking friends who you would be pulling along to all your nightly excursions."

"I feel a tear gathering behind my eyelids," Chex laughed, "you know me so well."

Phillip grunted. "I think I will spend my two months' vacation here instead. I want to see my vision for the west lawn come to life. I want to create a little space of unparalleled beauty."

"You're the managing director of a large company," Chex giggled. "You don't know anything about landscaping. Let a professional do it. Ask Jack; he is a professional landscaper."

"I can have Jack put my vision to paper," Philip said. "I'll just tell him what to do. I am not totally helpless when it comes to landscaping. I did transform mommy's old playground."

"To what end are you doing this?" Chex asked curiously.

"Well, I want to keep an eye on Pearl, and I want a vacation that I will find rewarding and fulfilling. I'll take a couple of books to read in the night, and indulge myself vicariously through the characters lives, that will be the extent of my adventures. You'll have to introduce me as Philip Knight, of course."

Chex howled with laughter. "So let me get this straight. You're going to do an undercover boss thing on Pearl? And you are going to pretend to be a gardener?"

"That's right," Philip said. "Well, in this case, a garden supervisor. I will act on Jack's directive. He will get the guys, source the flowers, and I'll be a figurehead."

"And this has nothing to do with the fact that you like Pearl and want to check her out?"

"Nothing," Philip said.

"You know you'd have a better chance as Philip Hastings because Pearl does not mess with the hired help. If you don't have money, Pearl won't be into you."

"We'll see about that," Philip said. "Just don't blow my cover, okay?"

"Okay," Chex chuckled. "This I have to see. So when will you start?"

"Next month," Philip said.

"I'll let her know that I will send a garden supervisor to redo the west lawn as per her recommendation." Chex laughed and hung up the phone.

Chapter Four

Pearl couldn't have thought of a better place to work. She had thought longingly of a nine-to-five job when she had managed Sensuous City, but this job was even better than that. Her responsibilities were not onerous. She was in charge of three housekeepers, three gardeners, four chefs, and three butlers. The rest of the services, like security, sales, and marketing, were subcontracted. Her job was to ensure that everything worked synergistically and that the guests were happy, and the property maintained.

Each of the luxe villas was named in Spanish: Azul, Verde, and Amarillo. Each had its own staff, who was quite adept at their job. Most of them had been there since the villas were built. She was the new kid on the block and was still learning the ins and outs of the operation.

So far, it was all manageable. They had automated booking and phone service. She dealt directly with the guests when they arrived, and so far, it was problem-free. She hadn't needed to intervene or put out any fires yet.

It was a dream job in a dream location. And she got to live in the manager's cottage, which was a mini-luxurious cottage. It reminded her of one of those villas she stayed in when she was a part of DJ Duke and Madge's entourage.

Added to the accommodations at the nice villa was a free lunch. The restaurant's chef, Chef Boyne catered lunch for all the staff. He sent out a menu and made the orders by ten o'clock. The food was good, and plenty, and Pearl had taken to saving some of her lunch for dinner. That way, she didn't have to cook if she didn't want to. It was a win-win.

Pearl headed to the office, a short five-minute walk from her cottage. The manager's cottage and the owner's cottage were close, only separated by a hedge of areca palms so thick she couldn't see over them. She had to walk the short pathway from her cottage to see next door.

To her knowledge, Chex was not going to be making use of the owner's cottage. She had it cleaned every day, though, and aired out.

She appreciated her morning treks to the office. Today there was not a cloud in the sky. Pearl felt like singing. She appreciated the sun on her face, the beauty of the hibiscus and other tropical plants that lined the stone pathway, and the fact that she was going to work at an exciting job. Every week so far was different and dynamic. They had a wedding scheduled for today and a surprise proposal by the west lawn gazebo.

The west lawn gazebo was the only fly in her ointment. It was the odd man out on an otherwise pristine property. She wished Chex would fix that area and make it pretty.

The west lawn aside, she felt productive, free, and blessed to work in a place like this.

She turned the corner and was met with the sign to the

admin office. No one would know it was an office if not for the sign. It was a round cottage made of brick and glass that was designed to blend into its environment.

The outside looked like a cozy house that was surrounded by flowers. It was straight out of a fairytale. The front entrance was framed by a rustic wooden porch with rocking chairs and potted plants scattered around.

The interior was cozy and charming, with wooden beams and exposed brick walls, giving the space a sense of rustic elegance.

The admin office was small but well-organized, with a reception desk, a few comfortable chairs for visitors, and a couple of workstations for the administrative staff, which was mainly her and Natalia, who doubled as both the concierge and her assistant.

Despite its compact size, the office was fully equipped with all the necessary technology and equipment to support the efficient running of the business.

There was a cubicle that the previous owner claimed as his; Pearl was contemplating removing it for added space.

Pearl swiped her card and went inside. Natalia was already at her desk. Natalia was a buxom woman in her late twenties. She had a sunny personality and was a perfect fit for the job. She could charm even the grumpiest guest into pleasantness.

Pearl had secretly watched her to learn how to handle difficult situations. She was sure that you couldn't go to school to get what Natalia had naturally, she was a pro with people. She had expected to get the management job when the previous manager had left, but that wasn't to be when Pearl came on the scene.

Sometimes Pearl felt bad that she had gotten the job instead, but not for long. She needed this.

She wasn't cut out to be a woman of leisure, to be Madge's sidekick forever. She was used to working and liked to pay her own way, which was ironic because she had always had a fantasy that she could be a lady who lunched.

At one time, she had fantasized that she could be a rich wife who met other rich wives, and they'd meet and go to the spa and do their hair and attend film premiers and music award shows.

But after nearly five months of living like that with Madge, she had to reassess that fantasy. She hated being idle. It just seemed like a waste of time.

"Hey Pearl," Natalia said when she walked into the office.

"Hey, Pearl said, "You're here early."

"Just a smidge early," Natalia said. "I'm leaving after lunch, remember?"

Pearl nodded. "Oh yes, you are going ring shopping with your boyfriend, soon-to-be husband."

"I am going to be a Mrs.!" Natalia squealed. "Oh, before I forget, Mr. Hastings called. He was on his way to bed and said you weren't answering your phone. He gave me a message for you. He said he's sending over a gardener to oversee the rehabilitation of the west side of the lawn in a month."

"Finally," Pearl said.

"The gardener will work out of the office here. He'll supervise the renovation of the gazebo and the reinventing of the lawn space. He will show you the landscape plan when he gets here."

"Good," Pearl nodded. "That's great news."

"And he will stay in the owner's cottage for the duration. Mr. Hastings is asking if you could please arrange everything for him."

"The owner's cottage, that's fancy," Pearl nodded. "No

problem whatsoever, I can't wait for that part of the property to be sorted out."

"He said the gardener was doing him a favor," Natalia said. "And we should give him everything he asks for."

Pearl made a face. "I hope the gardener doesn't come here and try to throw his weight around. While he doesn't impinge on my job, I won't impinge on his."

Natalia smiled. "I chuckled when I heard the gardener's name. I thought the both of you would go well together."

"Excuse me," Pearl sat in her chair. "What's his name?"

"Phil Knight," Natalia grinned. "And because you are Pearl Day, it's such a contrast. I'm looking forward to coming in here and saying, 'Good morning, Miss Day, and good morning, Mr. Knight.'"

Pearl groaned. Phillip, the handsome gardener? Her skin prickled just thinking about him.

"Admit it," Natalia said. "It has a nice ring to it, Knight and Day."

"It does have a certain something," Pearl replied with a smirk. "We'll see how well Mr. Knight and I get along. As long as he does his job and doesn't cause any trouble, we'll be just fine."

****

Philip walked into the admin office of El Cielo. It was just his luck that he had a pounding headache on his first day of moonlighting as a gardener.

"Good morning," he said to the ladies. They were both on the phone, and his eyes landed on Pearl immediately.

She looked up. He saw a hint of shock as she gazed at him, as if she didn't expect him and then she waved.

He waved back.

She was even prettier than he remembered. Her hair had grown since the last time he had seen her. It was in a bob cut, it covered her ear, and she had subtle streaks of red in it. She was gorgeous.

Were her lashes always that thick and long? Her lips always that generous? He thought. She wore lip gloss, and her tongue peeped out just a tiny bit to lick her lips.

She must have felt his stare. She looked at him and covered the phone. "Natalia will be with you in a moment."

He nodded. And I want you to be with me forever. Where did that thought come from? He wasn't feeling like himself. A dizzy wave was washing over him. He leaned on the reception desk, trying to center himself.

His head was pounding like a jack hammer, drilling at his head with a beat per second.

He was thankful that he had thought to use Chex's driver because he couldn't have shown up as a gardener in his high-end vehicle, and he couldn't have driven with this ache in his head.

"Oh, hello," Natalia Green got up from her desk and came over. "How may I assist?"

"I am Phil Knight," Phillip winced. He had to get used to being called Knight again. He hadn't been Phil Knight for twenty-one years. "I am the gardener."

"You are?" Natalia frowned. "You don't look like what I was expecting."

"Is that so?" Phillip asked weakly. He wanted to ask how a gardener was supposed to look. He ensured he wore his most worn jeans and a neutral shirt. In fact, his own gardener dressed better than this when he was out and about.

"Can I get the key to the cottage, please? I must take something for this headache and lie down somewhere dark."

"Yes, oh yes," Natalia said, lowering her voice. "My fiancé

has migraines, so I understand. Do you have tablets for it?"

"Just some regular over-the-counter pills," Phillip groaned, his lips barely moving.

Pearl hung up the phone and came over. "I'll walk with you to the cottage. You can leave your bags; I'll ask one of the guys to take them over."

"Thank you," Phillip said.

He could barely manage a smile, but even with the headache, the impact of her was still there.

She was concerned for him. That was nice to see. And she was kind.

He couldn't remember much of the walk to the cottage. He remembered that Pearl had put a steadying arm on his back. She had opened the door, led him straight to bed, and gave him the tablets from the side of his bag, that he had pointed out.

He didn't remember her leaving. He woke up a few hours later, and the ache was gone.

He looked around. He was in a room that was painted with neutral colors. The décor was decidedly tropical, with lots of browns and greens and exposed wood beams across the ceiling. There was a photo of two banyan trees directly across from the bed.

He looked at it for a while and decided to take a shower. He was feeling embarrassed. He had thought about seeing Pearl again, for a whole month.

That's all he had really focused on in the intervening weeks if he were to be honest. He had imagined that when he saw her again, he would be strong, dominant, and manly, but alas his headache had rendered him helpless and she had helped him to his cottage. That wasn't very manly, was it?

He could recall now the feel of her hand on his back as she looked at him with concern. She had even given him the medication that he had requested.

At least she had cared enough to see to his needs. Not bad for a person in hospitality or a person in general. He had to admit that she had seemed as if she really cared.

He got up and pulled the curtains. There was a patio door beyond the curtains, and beyond that was a patio area, and further out, a small pool. He stepped out and inhaled. Unfortunately, it wasn't as cool on the outside. The heat surprised him.

He stepped back inside. He didn't want to trigger another headache with the drastic temperature change.

What he needed was a shower and some food.

His bags were in the living room area, which was spacious and airy. There was a kitchen and dining area to one side and patio doors that opened to the pool.

He pulled all the curtains, had a shower, and was rummaging in the well-stocked pantry to fix himself something to eat when he heard a knock on the door.

He opened it. Pearl was standing there with a tray. "I was hoping you would be awake and that I wouldn't be disturbing you."

"I am awake." Phil looked at the tray. "Is that food?"

"Oh yes," Pearl nodded. "It's my lunchtime. Want to join me?"

"I can't think of a better offer." Phillip stepped aside to allow her to come in. She walked past him, and he sniffed her perfume. It was flowery and subtle. He liked it.

"How are you feeling?" Pearl laid out the containers on the table.

"Almost new." Phillip sat down across from her. "Thank you for helping me earlier."

"No problem," Pearl said. "You looked like you were going to keel over. I called Chex to find out if this was something that I should be worried about. He said he hadn't seen you with a headache since you were much younger. He said you got them all the time when you were stressed."

Phillip groaned. Chex mentioning that he knew him when he was younger, could have blown his cover.

"You two are pretty close, huh?" Pearl asked.

"We are." Phillip sighed. "We practically grew up together, though I am five years older than Chex."

"So, how did that work?" Pearl asked fascinatedly. "You were the gardener's son or something?"

"Actually, no. I am a farmer's son." Phillip said truthfully. "My father was abusive and had mental health problems. Mr. Hastings, Chex's grandfather, took me in when I was around nineteen years old. He showed me what true family life was like."

"Oh," Pearl murmured. "That was good of Mr. Hastings."

"He was the best," Phillip said. "He had one daughter, Chex's mother, but he was generous to the children in the community. He sent some to school, had some live with him in the mansion, and gave them jobs. The Hastings family is vast and not just blood relatives."

"Oh wow," Pearl murmured. "I wish there was a Mr. Hastings in my neighborhood when I was growing up."

"Why?" Phillip opened the food carton and looked at the food in anticipation. It was fish in a creamy sauce with noodles and roast vegetables.

"Well, my mother had eight of us. Only six of us survived. She lost two pregnancies after me. She was dirt poor. Sometimes she couldn't afford to send us to school. We couldn't afford basic necessities like food. Our clothes were hand-me-downs, and we always had a shoe shortage. We brushed our teeth with salt - you get the picture."

"I do," Phillip nodded.

"It was tough," Pearl opened her food and inhaled. "Fish and pasta, I love it. I don't know how the previous owner did it, but he got some good chefs to work here."

Phillip smiled. "He did. Your childhood sounded bad, but it wasn't worse than mine."

"Ha," Pearl took a bite of her food, chewed, and then swallowed. "We were so poor we lived in a one-room shack in a clearing. All of us couldn't hold in the cramped dwelling. Sometimes my two oldest brothers would have to take crocus bags and sleep outside under the trees."

"At least you slept," Phillip smirked. "I had to stay up and watch. My father would rotate us on four hour shifts like clockwork."

"What were you watching for?" Pearl asked, confused.

"The end of the world, according to my father's understanding. There would be a kind of zombie apocalypse. We couldn't be caught unawares."

Pearl chuckled. "You can't be serious."

"Quite serious. I wish we could have disappeared with a crocus bag and slept under trees; at least we'd be content, hoping to see another day instead of living on the edge with a hint of paranoia dogging our every move."

"Oh wow, I never knew there was someone out there who would envy us," Pearl said thoughtfully.

Phillip chuckled. "What is that saying? There is always someone worse off than you?"

"You were never worse off than me," Pearl insisted. "If you had food to eat, basic necessities, even a father figure, though he sounded loopy, you had more than I did."

"That's debatable," Phillip murmured. "What happened to your father?"

"My father killed someone in the middle of a robbery. He stabbed a shopkeeper several times while stealing bread of all the things. He was rightfully sent to jail," Pearl sighed. "My mother sure knew how to pick them. He was the only man who had actually stuck around for more than a year."

"My mother was cursed with attracting men who would promise her the world when they were having sex but ditched her when there was a baby. So she had four children for four different men, who all had the same playbook. And then my father came on the scene. He wasn't without his faults. He was always in and out of jail, but at least he stuck around long enough for my mother to have my older sister Precious and me."

"And then, when my father committed murder and was sent to jail for good, things got tougher. My mom started giving us away to people in the community who would have us. I stayed with Pastor Brewster and Lady Brewster in fits and spurts throughout my childhood. That's where I discovered the wonders of running water and toothpaste. I was ten when I first slept in a bed."

Phillip widened his eyes. "Okay, you win."

"I knew I would," Pearl said. "Added to my deprived childhood, I had a less than savory teenager phase, which saw me get pregnant at fifteen by a boy who said my child wasn't his. I saw shades of my mother happening all over again. And I said, nope, no way, am I going to go through the same thing again. I got smart right quick. My sister Precious was smart. She married rich."

"This explains a lot about you, Pearl." Phillip looked at her teasingly. "It also explains why you gave me that speech about caring for my children."

"I am so sorry about that." Pearl grinned. "You are a good-looking blue-collar worker. I made assumptions. Good-looking men in my sphere are never faithful to their wives or girlfriends; they have many kids all over town. They are always in high demand, stretched and pulled for every thirsty woman in their vicinity. And I liked you instantly, so I overreacted. That has never happened to me."

"You like me, huh?" Phillip grinned.

"I said 'liked' you," Pearl smiled. "Not 'like' as in currently happening."

"That's too bad because I like you too." Phillip smiled. "As in, instantly and currently. We should do something about it."

"Nope. We are not going to do anything about it," Pearl said firmly. "Now that we are in each other's vicinity, we should just agree on that."

"Because I am a gardener?" Phillip raised an eyebrow. "And not rich?"

"Something like that," Pearl said. "I have plans for my life. I don't want to spend the next phase of my life struggling like I did in the first phase. I need a forward-thinking, gainfully employed partner who is secure in the finance department."

"I am gainfully employed." Phillip sputtered. "And dare I say, forward-thinking."

"No offense was meant to you or your job," Pearl said. "But unless you have your own place and a side hustle or have some sort of plan, I am not interested."

"So, I don't have to be rich, just have a plan?" Phillip clarified.

"Well, maybe I'd make an exception for you but you have to have a place for yourself," Pearl said.

"Does living at the Hastings mansion count?" Phillip asked, grinning.

"No," Pearl said. "Where will you live when you are no longer working there as a gardener? Chex can kick you out any minute."

"I see your point," Phillip nodded. "But I doubt Chex will

ever kick me out. It's too much house for him alone."

Pearl glanced at her watch. "I have to go."

Phillip nodded.

"Don't let staying at the owner's cottage or your friendship with Chex make you think that you are coming here on some sort of vacation," Pearl said warningly. "You came here to sort out the west lawn. You better do it right. I am watching you."

"Yes, ma'am," Phillip said solemnly. He couldn't help himself; his eyes ran up and down her shapely derriere. He almost licked his lips. This woman was perfectly shaped and curvy in all the right places.

But he quickly snapped out of it and focused on the task at hand. He didn't want to spook her. He was there to monitor her to see if she was a right fit for his investment.

At least, that was the original story that he had accepted mentally.

"Don't worry, Pearl," he said with a professional tone. "I take my work seriously, and I'll make sure to do the job right. I'll stop by the office later with the plan to show you what I came up with for the west lawn."

"Good," Pearl said with a nod. "I'll see you later." She turned to leave but then paused and looked back at him. "And Phillip, just so we're clear, I don't mix business with pleasure."

Phillip raised an eyebrow, but he didn't argue.

"Understood," he said with a smirk.

He watched her leave.

He let out a low whistle as soon as she was out of sight. Being around Pearl would be a lot harder than he had originally thought.

Chapter Five

It was day two of seeing Phil Knight in the office. Pearl drummed her fingers impatiently on the desk. Why was he such a distraction? She was trying to figure out why he was so alluring to her? Was it the high cheekbones? His piercing stares? His deep pink lips? What was it?

He was currently frowning at the landscape plan, which was a good plan, by the way. It was cleverly done. She wondered why he was frowning. He was tracing his fingers slowly across the paper and jotting things down.

She found his actions almost hypnotic. Did he have to trail his fingers so slowly across the paper?

But then again, the man didn't have to do anything. He just needed to exist. Everything he did, she found suggestive or erotic. Her erogenous zones were in hyperdrive.

She should have followed through with her intent to get rid of the owner's cubicle that the previous owner had set up in the space. It faced the managers' desk fully.

Pearl was beginning to realize that it may have been by design. The previous manager and the owner had gotten married and left together.

It was a dreamy love story. He had hired her, and they had fallen in love, and when he returned to Spain, he brought her with him.

Why couldn't she have something like that?

And why was she so attracted to Phil Knight? She couldn't look up and risk her eyes connecting with his. He looked at her like he was hungry, and she was a last meal.

It both scared her and made her excited at the same time.

Nothing could go on between them. He was not the type of man that she had in her plans. He was a gardener who probably didn't have two cents to rub together and his only claim to stability was living with his employer, Chex in the Hastings Mansion.

If she kept telling herself that the days would sail by, he would return to Stony Hill and continue working for Chex as his gardener, and she would remain here at El Cielo.

Maybe one day, the ideal man of her dreams would appear. He would be single, maybe a businessman, or doctor or lawyer; he would take one look at her, and they would have the same kind of attraction she was feeling for Phillip right now.

She was being ridiculous. You couldn't replicate feelings; they were subjective, those pesky things. Besides, life did not go that way for the women in her family. Her daughter Jewel was a rare exception, and when her mother reconnected with Norman after many years, that was it.

As usual, thoughts of back home had her thinking about Leonard Crooks. If ever there was an antidote to her inexplicable feelings for Phillip, that was it.

Thoughts of Leonard and her precarious safety had taken

a backseat to the magnetizing presence of Phillip so far, but she couldn't ignore the specter of Leonard on her safety and survival.

Leonard was still out there, waiting for her to return to him. The longer she stayed away, the more he was probably plotting to get her to come back by whatever means necessary.

No one had managed to escape him, though some had certainly tried.

Mandy King had tried. She had crashed after her bachelorette party; Polly Dennis was seven months pregnant and had seemingly moved on when she drowned at her baby shower. Dania was preparing to migrate to the US when she too, mysteriously died from a heart attack after her farewell party.

Leonard had remarked to Pearl after hearing about the accidents, "It's funny how the women who leave me end up dead. Take note, Pearl, the angel of death works for me."

That's why Pearl had not taken a thing belonging to him. Nor did she want him to know where she was. That would be the end of it.

She wouldn't know where he would strike. She couldn't trust that he wouldn't hire someone to spike her drinks, mess with her brakes, or find some other creative way to get rid of her without getting his hands dirty, like he did with all those other women.

She signed a deal with the devil the day she started working for him and entered a relationship with him.

When he had said, with a serious look on his face, 'there is no escaping me, Pearl,' she had not thought the threat was serious.

How wrong had she been?

She got up. She needed some air. She also needed to do

her routine check when the guests vacated the villas. She grabbed her iPad, with her checklist, Villa Amarillo was empty and cleaned according to the housekeeper.

"I am going to check on Villa Amarillo," Pearl said out loud to Natalia who was busy jotting down something from her computer.

Natalia looked up. "While you are there, could you doublecheck that the water in the hot tub is back to being pure water and not beer?"

"Yes," Pearl said. "It's on my checklist and it was on the housekeepers too."

Phil looked up and frowned. "Someone really requested to soak in beer?"

"Oh yes," Natalia chuckled. "You should see some of the requests. Our next guest is a super-rich, super-exclusive client. She comes by twice a year for two weeks at a time. She only eats caviar for breakfast, truffle pizza for lunch, and filet mignon with truffle butter for dinner. She rarely varies from this. Her standard desserts are strawberry and cream and crème brûlée, and she has to be served aged champagne, not the new ones. She is a pain to shop for, and Chef Curtis said he is not driving around looking for the ingredients again, I should do it."

"I don't get the allure of truffle or caviar," Phillip said. "I do like crème brûlée, though."

"Have you had it before?" Both Pearl and Natalia asked at the same time.

"Yes," Phillip nodded. "Don't look so impressed. Caviar is fish eggs, and truffle is a fungus that tastes like rancid mushrooms to me. And before you think only rich people can afford it, there are several price points for both of them that are not worth it, in my humble opinion. As for crème brûlée, it's just five ingredients. Cheesecake tastes better to me."

"That's because you don't have rich-honed taste buds," Natalia said.

"That might be true," Phillip chuckled. "I am most times unimpressed with the things that I hear that rich people like. But then again, I am a man of simple tastes. I like good food, fine wine, aged or not, and a willing woman who loves me and will be by my side through thick and thin, rich or poor."

Pearl cleared her throat. She didn't know why he was looking at her when he was saying all of that. "I am off to Villa Amarillo."

"Before you go," Natalia said, "there is a mix-up."

"What?" Pearl frowned.

"Remember our truffle lady? Her name is Madam Lafon. They booked her into Villa Verde instead of Villa Azul. She won't like this," Natalia fretted, "she is a creature of habit. Everything has to be done to her liking or she'll drive the staff crazy. She is a stickler when it comes to certain things."

"I'll sort it out," Pearl said, "when I get back."

"She arrives tomorrow, Azul is booked, and honeymooners will be in there," Natalia said, "The most you can do is grovel tomorrow when she comes and says she is in the wrong villa. Hope that she has her toy boy with her, and he is a good one. She seems to pick the men at random. The more into them, she is, the less picky she gets with the staff."

"Okay, I'll grovel," Pearl said, "I will cry if needs be. I will make her forgive us for the mix-up."

She walked to the door and saw Phillip smiling.

She didn't need his approval. But somehow, she craved it. What was going on with her and this guy?

She shook her head, trying to push those thoughts away. She had more pressing matters to attend to, like fixing the mix-up with the truffle lady's villa.

"Good luck with the groveling," Phillip said, smiling. "Somehow, you don't strike me as a good groveller."

"I am not," Pearl sighed, "I am going to have to check my How to Grovel book."

"I can give you lessons," Phillip winked, "groveling is both an art and a science. The key is to do it without seeming to. I'll clear my schedule for you all day if I have to."

Pearl smirked, "I'll take a raincheck on that."

She exited the office feeling exhilarated by their exchange. Even their banter excited her on a level she couldn't comprehend. She tried to shake the thought and focused on her current task.

As she arrived at Villa Amarillo, Pearl pulled out her iPad and started to do her routine checks. She walked around the property, checking everything from the air conditioning to the hot tub. Once done, she made a note on her iPad and returned to the main office.

On her way back, Pearl couldn't help but think about the truffle lady and the upcoming situation. She knew this guest would be a challenge, but she was determined to make it right. She made a mental note to research the guest's preferences and ensure everything was perfect for her stay.

When she arrived at the office, Pearl saw that Phillip was no longer there. She felt a small pang of disappointment but quickly pushed it aside. She had work to do.

Chapter Six

Pearl headed toward Villa Verde apprehensively. She wasn't looking forward to dealing with Madame Lafon. If what Natalia said was true, this was going to be her very first test as manager. She had to do a good job. Both Philip and Natalia were watching to see how she would handle this. She didn't want to seem incompetent.

She stood on the steps of the villa, her heart slightly pounding. Howard, the butler, stood beside her. She had switched the butler and staff from Azul to Verde to accommodate Madame Lafon.

"Now she's a tough cookie," Howard said beside her. "I think the only problem you'll have convincing her to stay at this villa is that the pool is on the left at Villa Azul, and it's on the right here."

Pearl grimaced. "So, she takes those kinds of things into consideration?"

"Oh, yes," Howard said. "She's been coming here now for

five years. It seems the only change she likes is the young men she takes as companions."

"She's sounding scarier by the minute," Pearl said.

Howard laughed. "She's really not that bad. Apart from having very specific ways of doing things, she doesn't interact with us much. So sorry I can't help you more, Miss Pearl."

"No problem," Pearl said. "You have been helpful."

The town car stopped at the entrance to the villa. The driver got out and opened the back door. Madame Lafon stepped out. She wore fashionable dark glasses that seemed to cover her whole face, and she was in a stylish beige caftan that had red patterns at the front.

She had a glowing dark brown complexion, from what Pearl could see under a beige straw hat that matched her dress, and she was wearing braids with colorful red beads at the end. With a name like Madam Lafon, Pearl had not been expecting braids. However, her bearing was exactly what Pearl had imagined a rich, pampered woman to look like.

She walked down the steps toward Madame Lafon.

"This is the wrong villa," Madam Lafon said as she paused at the car door as if she was going back in. "I always stay at Azul."

There was something about her voice, her whole demeanor.

Pearl moved closer to her. There was something familiar with this woman. If you removed the glasses and the accent, she might resemble a younger version of her mother.

"Excuse me, Madam Lafon," Pearl cleared her throat, "I am sorry, but there was a mix-up with the booking. Villa Azul is currently occupied. Villa Verde has the same amenities, and I transferred over the staff you are used to. They are looking forward to..."

Madam Lafon removed her glasses and widened her eyes.

"Pearl, what on earth are you doing here?"

Pearl stilled. "Precious?"

The driver, who was eagerly poised to see how Pearl would handle the mix-up, straightened up and looked intrigued.

Pearl bit back a smile. He probably didn't expect this, and neither had she. "I am the new manager here. I came to apologize for the mix-up with the villas. I didn't know you were Madam Lafon."

"Oh, come here!" Precious said, enveloping her in a hug. "I can't believe this. I haven't seen you for too many years to count. My sweet baby sister."

Pearl was shocked on many levels. She hadn't anticipated this, least of all Precious calling her, her sweet baby sister. "How many years has it been since I last saw you?" Precious exclaimed.

"About twenty-one and some months," Pearl said. She knew the exact time. She had been fifteen and pregnant, and Precious had been nineteen and pissed at her for ruining her life.

"I'll make do with Villa Verde," Precious said. "I can't believe this. This is a good sign."

The driver started to take the bags out of the trunk.

"Er…do you have anyone accompanying you?" Pearl asked awkwardly.

"Nope," Precious said. "I came to think and do some reassessment of my life. It's a sign that you are here now. You are a part of that reassessment."

Pearl inhaled shakily, and to say she was shocked was an understatement.

The butler came for the bags. "Greetings Madam Lafon. It is lovely to see you again."

"Greetings Howard," Precious said breezily. She headed up the stairs, and Pearl walked behind her.

"We must do lunch today," Precious looked across at Pearl. "We have a lot of catching up to do."

"We do," Pearl nodded. "It's such a surprise to see you. You look so much like Mama."

"Yes, I do, with just a dash of Papa," Precious nodded. "And you, you are all Papa. Somehow, I had imagined that you would be looking hard and broken down. But my goodness, you are still fresh-faced and gorgeous. Your looks have not declined. You need to tell me your secret."

Pearl grinned. "Thank you. I wish I had a secret. It's all in the genes. You don't look too bad yourself."

"Don't be nice to me," Precious stopped. "I have been horrible to you. Besides, the toll my life has taken on me is bound to be showing. No amount of spa appointments can hide that."

"But whenever we've talked in recent years, you've been so happy. Everything is going well in your world."

"Ha," Precious made a face, "Pearl, I have been lying to you, trying to put on a brave face. The truth is, things have been tough for me. We'll talk at lunch. When is your lunchtime?"

"One," Pearl said.

"Well, see you at one then," Precious smiled and walked into the villa. "Oh wow, this is lovely!"

****

Pearl went back to the office, her mind racing.

"How did it go?" Natalia asked.

"Surprisingly well," Pearl said. "Madame Lafon turns out to be someone I know."

"That's good," Natalia said. "That means she didn't give you a hard time."

"Not at all. In fact, she hugged me and called me her baby sister. I'll be having lunch with her at one."

"Get out!" Natalia screamed, "she is your sister! As in blood sister?"

Pearl nodded. "I haven't seen her in twenty-one years, though."

Pearl looked down at the desk. There was a single yellow rose and a small envelope beside it.

"This is pretty," she murmured.

"That's what I told him," Natalia said.

"Him?" Pearl opened the envelope.

It was a note from Philip with a poem. Your presence fills my heart with delight, Like the yellow rose that shines so bright. Your warmth and kindness, like its hue, bring happiness to all I do. And so, I ask, with a smile on my face, can we have dinner at my place?

He was poetic, and it was a unique dinner invitation. Pearl smiled. He had barely been in the office. Yesterday he came in to say hi and then spent most of his day, she assumed, by the gazebo. They were laying out the plans for where to put what flowers, and it seemed like it excited him. If she didn't know better, she would think that this wasn't something he did often. How on earth could he still be so excited about his job?

It was a gift to be so enamored with your work that it didn't feel like work at all. Pearl couldn't help but admire his passion, and it was evident in everything he did, from the way he spoke about the garden and his roses to the twinkle in his eyes as he talked about his plans. She was intrigued by this man, who seemed to live and breathe nature.

"He's courting you," Natalia said, noticing the faraway look on Pearl's face.

"Uh huh," Pearl nodded. "I have never gotten a rose and

a dinner invitation poem from a guy."

"Poetry? That's so sweet. Is it any good?"

"I think so, but I don't know much poetry except roses are red, violets are blue," Pearl said, "and I don't know if it's a good idea to go to dinner with him."

"I would date him in a heartbeat," Natalia said, "if I didn't have Nathan and if he was interested in me, that is. He's hot and intelligent. I overheard him talking on the phone with someone, and he sounded like he was in charge."

"Is that so?" Pearl asked. "Was it about roses? He knows his plants, I tell you."

"Nope, it sounded like he was discussing a legal matter." Natalia laughed. "Anyway, if I were you, I would cease the chance to be with him. When the two of you are in the office, you don't have eyes for anyone else. That's what you call heightened attraction."

Pearl grunted. "I don't know about that, and I am not sure what he is thinking with this."

"Maybe you can get a clue from the rose color," Natalia said, "every rose color has a meaning. I am sure that he knows that."

"Is that so?" Pearl picked up the single-stemmed yellow rose and inhaled it. It had a light fruity scent.

"It's true. I found that out when I was looking around for what I would put in my bridal bouquet. I even had a handy list here that I got from the florist. I was thinking of doing a mixture for the symbolism. Nathan thinks I am being ridiculous because no one cares or knows about the symbolism, but guess what? I do." Natalia rummaged in her bag and came up with her list. "Here it goes. Yellow means friendship."

"Friendship?"

"Isn't that sweet," Natalia beamed. "He wants to be

friends. At least for now, that's always a good place to start."

But that's the thing, Pearl thought she didn't know if she wanted to start. She sensed that Phillip was different. For starters, he wasn't like any of the men she knew and her reaction to him was not comparable to any other man.

She was trying to qualify what the allure was. There would be absolutely nothing wrong with them being friends. But she didn't trust herself around him. She was now in unchartered waters. She had never been so attracted to a man.

She was so physically aware of him; it was affecting her sanity. It was scary and exciting at the same time.

But it was just dinner. What's the harm in going to dinner? She would make up her mind later. For now, she didn't know what she would say.

****

One o'clock sneaked upon her with the suddenness of a surprise visitor. Pearl glanced at the clock on her computer screen and sighed. She had been so engrossed in sorting out the details for the two events that would be held at the property that weekend that she had lost track of time.

She would have to take her phone; one of the event planners was a nervous wreck, and her jumpy anxiety was beginning to affect Pearl.

She had a lunch date with Precious Day, aka Madam Lafon, and she was running a bit late. She partially dreaded and anticipated talking to her sister.

They spoke on the phone occasionally these last couple of years, but it was mostly to talk about Jewel and her schooling.

Precious had graciously paid for her housing for her entire

time at university. It had gone a long way into helping them out, and Pearl had been grateful.

There was so much about Precious that Pearl didn't know. She hadn't even known her last name, her husband's name, or what happened to her after she married him and left Jamaica. She didn't even know if Precious had children. It was appalling how much she didn't know about her sibling. They had once been close, even though there was a four-year age gap between them, Precious had been a cool, caring big sister when they were younger, and Pearl had idolized her.

It had all ended when Precious returned from school for the holiday and heard that Pearl was no longer living with the family.

Their mother had found out she was pregnant, had zero tolerance for an extra mouth to feed, and had told Pearl to leave.

Everything she owned was packed in a black plastic bag. Her mother had handed it to her and said, "I am not mad, just disappointed. Let the Webbs deal with this; they have money. You are their problem now."

Except the Webbs would have been willing to help, but her boyfriend, Darnell — the imbecile who had convinced her, despite her better judgment, that the withdrawal method of birth control was foolproof — had told them that the baby wasn't his.

At first, he had blamed her pregnancy on his brother, David.

Unfortunately for Pearl, she had unwittingly praised and acted starstruck over David one too many times in Darnell's presence.

And mainly because of David's new car. She had been car mad at the time, and so was David. To Darnell, chatting with his brother and getting a lift in his car occasionally meant she was cheating. It had been the excuse that he needed to deny paternity, and his parents had taken a wait-and-see approach.

They had all treated her as if she was some kind of loose woman who had gotten pregnant alone.

She had been left homeless with only a single bag with all her worldly belongings and nowhere to go.

She had seriously considered jumping off the bridge at Cascade Hills. Luckily, it hadn't come to that. While wandering aimlessly in the community, Pastor Jeff Brewster and his wife Eugenia had been driving by and stopped. They had offered her a ride and listened patiently to her story. They had taken her in and given her a place to stay, offering her support and encouragement.

She had stayed with them before.

When she was ten, she and Precious spent an entire summer with them. Eugenia had been impressed to take them from the home after visiting and seeing the substandard conditions they lived in.

Their mother had been in the hospital with yet another pregnancy, and her oldest brother, Martin, had been in charge of his younger siblings. It had not been a pretty sight.

Eugenia stepped in for Pearl again. She ensconced Pearl in one of the guest rooms and acted like a surrogate parent and supporter. Both Eugenia and Jeff had been brilliant.

Precious had heard that she was staying with the Brewsters and, thinking nothing of it, had visited her sister.

When she saw Pearl's belly, she was livid.

Pearl winced at that recollection of the exchange twenty-one years later.

She remembered it like it was yesterday. Why were some memories so vivid, and yet others faded into obscurity?

"You are going to end up like Mama!" Precious had

shouted. "This is it, the beginning of the end, for you. You will be the plaything for all the men in the community. They'll give you baby after baby, and in a few years, when your looks fade, and you have a string of children, no one will want you."

Pearl cowered in the corner of the room, hunching over as far as she could with her rounded belly. Every word was like a hammer on her head.

"You couldn't even wait to finish high school!" Precious yelled. "What's wrong with you? Haven't you seen how we have lived over the past couple of years? Is this really something you had wanted to take on, Pearl?"

Pearl shook her head. She couldn't even speak. The shame was so great.

"You don't have two cents to rub together. The baby's father wants nothing to do with you, and here you are. How could you be so cruel to carry another mouth to feed in this situation?"

Pearl started to cry. This, above all, had been her regret. She was dooming this baby to failure and a life of poverty and needs. This wasn't anything she hadn't told herself before.

Precious sat on the bed across from her. "You should have gotten an abortion," she said.

Pearl looked up at her miserably. "The thought never crossed my mind. I know I am not in the best position right now, but I want her."

Precious snorted. "I never want kids. It's cruel to carry them into this world and live like this. Give it away."

"The baby is a girl, not it," Pearl sniffed.

"This baby will ruin your life; stop defending it." Precious sighed. "And to think you were so bright and quick to learn things, and you are such a pretty girl, prettier than Opal or me, you could have modeled. It's all wasted now. Now you're a single mother. Who is going to want you?"

"You were supposed to save yourself for a rich upstanding man who would elevate you in some way. Instead, you settled for the dregs. You messed up your life, Pearl. You should have done like me. You should have gotten a higher education and found a man with money. Now here you are, stuck with a kid. I'm done with you, Pearl."

Precious got up. "You are dead to me. All of you, including Mama, make me sick. I can't believe I had the misfortune to be born in a family like ours."

And she had kept true to her words until Jewel entered university.

****

Precious decided to have lunch on the patio.

"It's nice here," Precious said. "Verde has a unique charm. I don't know why I was so set on Azul."

Pearl smiled. "You have never liked change."

"That's so true," Precious sighed. "First things first, how is Jewel? I try to keep in touch with her monthly, but we are slacking off. She's so busy these days with her new career and husband."

"And house," Pearl said proudly. "She moved into her new house last week. They had a housewarming party. She sent me a video."

"Why didn't you go?" Precious asked.

"I am hiding out from Leonard. He is not pleased that I left Sensuous City."

"That man is dangerous," Precious said. "Some stories were floating around about him and how he started out in business from back in the day. I was surprised to find out that you spent so much time working for him.”

“I did it for survival,” Pearl said. “I was nineteen with a three-year-old. I couldn't burden the Brewsters anymore. They helped me out a lot. They went above and beyond for me, even though I am not family.”

“When your own family had pushed you away,” Precious sighed, “I could have helped.”

“I am not blaming you for anything,” Pearl said. “And technically, I wasn't pushed away. Mama still helped. When she married Norman, she helped even more. Opal got a good job at a hotel in Cayman and faithfully sent money to help with the baby. And both Martin and Mason were always sending me produce from their farm. Gabe had too many children at that time to help me out, but Jewel got all the cute hand-me-downs that his wife could find from her children. I got by.”

Precious frowned. “So, in other words, I was the only one that didn't help?”

“You had distanced yourself from all of us by then,” Pearl shrugged. “Life went on without you.”

“I could have done something,” Precious sighed. “I was so caught up in not wanting anything to do with my origins I allowed myself to forget how close we were as siblings. A closeness borne out of the worst type of poverty, but we were close, nevertheless. I didn't once reach out and do something to help any of you, and I had the means to do it. I feel so awful about it. I sometimes think what I am going through is karma, some kind of punishment somehow. Isn't there something in the Bible about helping your family first?”

Pearl shrugged. “I don’t know.’“

“If I had helped, you wouldn't have worked with Leonard. If I had helped, Mama would have her own place now and wouldn't have been caught up in the war of the Crooks family spoils. If I had helped, Martin and Mason would have owned their farm much sooner. Gabe wouldn't be working on a series of dead-end jobs, and Opal, well Opal is alright. She really worked herself ragged and put herself through school."

"It's all in the past," Pearl tried to reassure her. "I worked with Leonard, and I ended up leaving. What he does after this is another matter. Our brothers are all doing fine. They are much better than when we were younger. Gabe only struggles because he is sending two children through college, and he did say you helped with that. As for Mama, she is living her best life in Cayman. She lives with Opal and her husband and takes care of her grandchildren. The family as a whole is thriving despite our initial challenges."

"Mama says that all the time," Precious said forlornly. "It seems as if I am the only one in our family that's not thriving."

"Why would you say that?" Pearl asked.

Precious looked down at the table. "My marriage is over. To be honest, it hadn't really begun. I was living in a bubble, pretending that everything was alright. I thought marrying a rich man was the ultimate goal, but..."

"But what?" Pearl leaned into the table.

"It's hard," Precious said. "It's lonely. The only thing that gets him excited is money. He thinks all I need to do is throw dinner parties to enhance his business interests and sit and look pretty. We go places, but it's for business. We have friends, but they are strategic relationships, all for the good of the business.

"I have no real connection with anyone. And when we are alone, he doesn't even bother to talk to me. He's always on his phone or computer, focused on work or investments. I feel like I'm just an accessory in his life. When I complain, he asks me how I think we can afford all the nice things if he doesn't work for them.

"He is cold and distant," Precious sniffed. "And he says I am too whiny and needy. He doesn't understand me or seem to care about my feelings. I have tried to make it work, but I feel trapped."

"I don't know what to do. I thought I had everything I wanted, but now I have nothing. Marrying a super-rich power broker of a husband was a mistake."

Pearl gasped. "Really?"

"He who feels it knows it," Precious sighed. "If I could do it all again, I would marry someone with moderate means, maybe someone with a tiny cottage near the sea. Someone who lives close to nature. We could grow our own food, have a dog and a cat, and maybe a baby. I have gotten broody lately."

Pearl raised her eyebrows. "So why haven't you divorced him then?"

"I can't initiate a divorce. I won't get much money. I try to goad him into initiating the proceedings by having affairs with all sorts of people, but the man is unmoved," Precious sighed. "I signed a pesky little prenup that says if I initiate a divorce, I get a small sum. I didn't put up with his misogyny and conceit, not to mention his little jibes at my weight, hair, and clothes, for twenty-one years just to end up with a mere pittance."

"What do you call a mere pittance?" Pearl asked.

"A million dollars," Precious sniffed. "He is worth many more millions than that."

"A million US dollars?" Pearl whistled. "You are snuffing at a million dollars when you could have freedom? You could start a business with that, buy a house or two…."

"But I am not as brave as you are," Precious sighed. "I am a coward at heart. I fear being broke again."

"A million dollars is not broke," Pearl said. "And you can't have the cottage by the sea and the moderately successful man if you are tied to the one you have now."

Precious nodded. "I hear you."

"I can't get over the fact that for all these years, I have been envying you marrying rich when it was all a lie," Pearl whispered.

"It's all just smokes and mirrors. I couldn't bear for you to think that I was to be pitied," Precious said. "I have discovered true luxury is having genuine love, trust, and respect in a relationship. It's about being yourself and feeling truly valued for who you are, not just for what you can gain materially."

Pearl nodded contemplatively.

"My fortieth birthday is later this year, and what have I accomplished, Pearl? Nothing. I flitter around the world. I spend my husband's money, and I have had too many affairs. I've been everywhere, partied with celebrities, and attended their award shows. I have friends who you wouldn't believe. But deep inside, I'm still lonely. And I'm worse off than all of my siblings. At least all of you have families. I have no one."

"You still have us," Pearl said. "All you need to do is get back in touch."

"I don't know," Precious murmured. "I feel guilty for not being there. Too many years have passed for me to waltz back into your lives. I envy your relationship with Jewel. She's such a caring, concerned child. She said you told her to marry rich because of me," Precious laughed. "Oh Pearl, if nineteen-year-old me could go back in time, I would tell myself to marry whoever makes you happy. And I would apologize for saying those appalling things to you. I am happy you had Jewel. I am happy you didn't give her away, and I am so sorry about those awful things I said."

"You are forgiven," Pearl blinked back tears. It had taken her sister twenty-one years, but there it was, the apology. "When you offered to help Jewel, I knew you were sorry about the things you said."

"I was more than sorry. I was sorry the minute I said it. Are you seeing anyone?" Precious asked curiously changing the subject.

"Well, kind of," Pearl said. "I have an interest in someone. He likes me too. I don't know where it is going."

"All I have to say is pursue what makes you happy," Precious said. "Don't be like me."

"You still have time to correct your mistakes, Precious. You're thirty-nine. You can get that divorce and start all over again."

"I don't know, Pearl," Precious said. "That's what this trip is about, some well-needed introspection."

The chef carried the food, and the topic changed to other things. At the back of Pearl's mind, throughout the lunch, was Precious' advice, pursue what makes you happy.

The thought of Phillip made her happy. She would never think of him as just the gardener again. She wouldn't judge any future prospects for a relationship based on the man's wealth. That was foolhardy and shallow. What mattered was how he made her feel, and Phillip made her feel happy and alive.

After lunch, Pearl hugged Precious goodbye. As she watched her disappear into the villa, Pearl couldn't help but feel a twinge of sadness. Despite their rocky relationship, Precious was still her sister, and it had been good to see her again.

But now, Pearl had something to look forward to. Ironically, Precious's honesty gave her a new perspective on life and love. She was ready to take a chance on Phillip.

She walked back to the office; she couldn't help but smile at the thought of seeing him again.

When she reached the office, he wasn't there. Pearl called his number and waited for him to answer.

"Hello?" his voice came through the line.

"Hi, Phillip, it's Pearl," she said, trying to keep the excitement out of her voice.

"Hi, Pearl. How was lunch with Madam Lafon?"

"It was good," Pearl said. "I got your dinner invite. Yes, I'll have dinner with you tonight."

There was a pause on the other end of the line before Phillip answered, "Looking forward to it."

"By the way, I love your poetry," Pearl said, "you are quite creative."

Phillip laughed. "It's a new hobby. I spend hours thinking of how I can put it together to impress you."

"Well, I am impressed," Pearl chuckled. "See you later."

Chapter Seven

"**W**elcome to Chateau Knight," Phillip greeted Pearl at the door when she showed up for dinner.

She laughed. "Does this mean we are going to have French food?"

Phillip smiled. "We are."

"Well, I am happy. I dressed for the occasion." She had decided to wear a flowing floral maxi dress and had taken extra care with her makeup.

Phillip chuckled. "You always look lovely, Pearl, but tonight you look especially beautiful. You're going to fit right in with the theme."

"Thank you, Sir Knight," Pearl smiled. "You don't look too bad yourself."

He was dressed in a black t-shirt and jeans that molded his hips lovingly. Pearl dragged her eyes from his jeans and up to his face. He smiled at her like he knew what she was thinking.

"So you slaved away in the gardens all day and still managed to cook French cuisine?" Pearl said, her voice slightly breathless.

Phillip laughed. "I can't take credit for the food. I had it catered by Chef Boyne."

"That's extravagant," Pearl looked at him. "I know Chef Boyne does private catering on the side, and he's expensive. Natalia wanted to use him for her wedding but couldn't afford him."

"Ah," Phillip nodded. "Not to worry, he didn't charge me a thing. I did him a favor, and the man refused to take payment. He says he owes me."

"What did you do?" Pearl asked, intrigued.

"I put in a good word for him, and his wife got a job at one of the Hastings companies today."

"Oh my," Pearl looked at him speculatively. "You have that much clout?"

"It seems as if I do," Phillip smiled. "I have been around a long time and made some friends in the Hastings group of companies."

Pearl smiled. "Okay."

She belatedly heard the music playing in the background. It was Roberta Flack's, 'The First Time Ever I Saw Your Face.' He even had impeccable taste in music."

"I like that song," Pearl said. "I love that era of music. The seventies, eighties, and nineties had some really good songs."

"I do, too," Phillip nodded. "Chex thinks I am a dinosaur. I didn't even know about your friend DJ Duke. Apparently, he is all the rage right now."

Pearl laughed. "He is. His music is different, still enjoyable, but I think the seventies to nineties era is filled with nostalgia for me."

"Me too." Phillip indicated to the table. "I hope you are hungry. I had Chef Boyne do a three-course French menu, which he said he could do in his sleep. For starters, we have French Onion Soup: a rich, flavorful soup made with caramelized onions and beef broth and topped with melted Gruyere cheese and a crispy baguette crouton. The main course is Coq au Vin, a chicken braised in red wine with mushrooms and pearl onions. Served with mashed potatoes. And for dessert, inspired by the fact that you have never had it- crème brûlée: a creamy, custard dessert with a crispy caramelized sugar topping."

"Oh goodness," Pearl licked her lips. "I am impressed."

Phillip chuckled. "To finish the meal, I have some relaxing rose tea brewing."

The dinner had surpassed expectations, and Pearl ate every morsel on her plate.

They moved to the patio after dinner and sat in adjoining lounge chairs. The evening was balmy, with a light breeze. And it smelled delightful. Phillip had bundles of roses in buckets out there.

So this is where her daily rose gift came from.

"Oh, before I forget, I have to get the tea. It's a perfect way to top off dinner."

She looked in the cup after he served the tea. She had never had rose tea. "Are you sure roses are edible?" Pearl looked into the teacup.

Phillip laughed. "It is. Trust me. I have had it countless times."

Pearl took a tentative sip. It was delicious.

"So, tell me about your visit with Madam Lafon." Phillip was a good conversationalist. She didn't know how he did it, but she was talking about her life and sharing stuff she couldn't remember sharing before. Like how tough it had been with Jewel in the early years. How hard it was for her to juggle taking high school classes while working at Sensuous City. And finally, she had gone on about her disbelief that Precious wasn't happy with her life.

"I still can't believe she is unhappy. I ordered my life, thinking Precious was the opposite of me. She got her education, married a rich man, and wasn't a pregnant teenage mother struggling to make ends meet. Only to find out that her life was nothing to envy."

Pearl took a sip of her tea. "Jewel is going to laugh at me when she hears this. I grew up that child telling her to marry a rich man and not be like me. And today, I found out that I was wrong. So wrong. I am happy she didn't listen to me."

"It sounds like, despite your innate biases, you didn't do too bad a job with her," Phillip said.

"It's been staring me in the face, and I didn't get it," Pearl said faintly. "I have never met a rich man who was truly contented. They are always about money and their businesses, and their toys. Many of them have no time to spend with their spouse. They have so many options, with people throwing themselves at them. How can they be faithful?"

"Wait a minute," Phillip said hoarsely, "you do know that not everyone is the same, don't you?"

"Don't defend them," Pearl said heatedly. "I have been looking at this all wrong. My stepbrother Leonard is rich, obsessed with money and power, and never satisfied with what he has. He's always striving for more at the expense of his happiness and those around him. Because he has money, he treats people like trash. I don't want that kind of life. I want to focus on what really matters, on building strong relationships and living a fulfilling life, rather than chasing after wealth and status. Money may be important, but it's not everything. I've learned that the hard way."

"Look at Precious. She has all the wealth in the world, and she is miserable. Money really can't buy happiness, can it? I wish I had realized this earlier. I wish I had encouraged Jewel to follow her dreams, find her passions, and live a life that makes her happy, rather than trying to fit into society's narrow definition of success. I failed her in that regard."

Phillip cleared his throat. "Pearl, not to pour cold water on your epiphany, but you are doing it again."

"What?" Pearl asked.

"You are using your sister's experiences to judge a whole group of people. When you thought she was rich and happy, you aspired to find a rich man so that you could be just as happy, but now you found that it was fake, you are lumping all rich men into the mold of cold and distant. There are exceptions to every rule. Mr. Hastings was rich, and he was a loving family man that was accessible and loving and found time for people.

Pearl nodded. "You are right. I generalize too much. DJ Duke is rich, and he finds time for Madge. But then again, he is always on the road. If she wants to see him, she has to follow him around. I did that for four months, and I hated it. The excitement of going somewhere new wears off. I guess I am a homebody at heart. Precious is right. A man of moderate means in a cottage in the country is my new aspiration."

Phillip frowned. He didn't want Pearl to be turned off from him when he finally told her that he was really Phillip Hastings, head of the Hastings Group of Companies, who by the age of thirty had doubled his grandfather's considerable wealth. There had been times when he didn't see the value in stopping and smelling the roses; his relationships had indeed been an afterthought. Helena had not minded the status quo; she had been busy too.

But he didn't want that kind of setup with Pearl. He wanted something different. He wanted a fulfilling life and finding joy in the simple things. The past few days moonlighting as a gardener had shifted something in him.

"All of today has been an eye-opener," Pearl murmured.

"For me, too," Philip sipped his tea. It was just their first date, and already he was thinking that what he felt for her was the real deal.

"This tea is making me mellow and relaxed."

"That's the power of rose tea," Philip said. "I remember my first taste of rose tea. My mom always made it, especially after a particularly tough day with my dad. I remember he would be ranting about something, anything. The smallest thing could set him off, and then my mom would sit down and calmly drink her rose tea. Sometimes it would be rosehips. It made her calmer; she would offer me some, and I would feel the anxiety floating away with each sip."

"Funnily enough, I know about rosehips," Pearl said, "my grandmother drank it for joint pains. I didn't know it was a part of the rose plant."

"It is," Phillip said. "I think my mother is the one who made me appreciate roses. They are not just pretty; they are useful."

Pearl chuckled. "You know I have to hand it to you. You're really dedicated to your gardening."

"I love it," Philip said.

"I envy that," Pearl said.

He looked at her. "What do you ultimately want to do?"

"I want to go to college," Pearl mused. "Probably not full-time; there are so many online options these days. I'd probably do social work. I think I have a calling with that. That's the one thing I miss about Sensuous City. I helped the girls there. I counseled them when they needed it. So many girls go to that place hopeless and desperate, looking for a job and grasping at straws. There were too many days where I had to talk them out of doing drugs, sleeping with men who would just mess up their lives and making the same old mistakes that got them there in the first place."

Philip nodded. "It's a pity some of us don't learn from our parent's mistakes."

"I didn't," Pearl snorted. "I got pregnant at fifteen. My mom had gotten pregnant at fourteen. I think she was too busy trying to survive life to keep up with me. You know what I'd do? Pearl turned to Philip. I'd open a place of safety for girls. Run a charity. Make a practical difference in people's lives. And if I had the chance to do it all again, be in a steady, committed relationship and have a child or two.

"I didn't do too badly with Jewel. I may have been a bit too strict, but to tell you the truth, I don't regret it. Why am I telling you any of this? What about your hopes and dreams?"

"Well, I," Philip laughed uncomfortably, "I'd like to help people too, obviously, like Mr. Hastings did when he took me in. I'd also like to invest in a greenhouse specializing in roses. Nobody had what I wanted in the quantity that I required when I was sourcing the plants to put in the west garden."

"Ah," Pearl nodded. "That's a great idea. You really love your roses."

"I do," Philip nodded. "I think my rose garden at Stony Hill has kept me sane."

"Don't you mean Chex's rose garden?" Pearl asked.

"Technically," Philip shrugged. "But I landscaped it, built it from scratch. Even he knows it's mine. He calls it Phil's Garden."

"Has he even seen it?" Pearl asked. "Chex doesn't strike me as a flower garden type of guy."

"He is not," Philip chuckled. "And yes, he's seen it once."

"Where on the grounds do you live?" Pearl asked. "The place is so huge."

"I live on the second floor with Chex," Philip said. "The top floor has its own entrance, so it is rented out. There is a helper's suite on the ground floor, a three-bedroom apartment that various family members stay in when they come to Jamaica, and a fully equipped gym. And, of course, there are four other cottages on the grounds. That's where the drivers and the security and the gardeners stay."

Pearl widened her eyes. "Really? You live in the main house? Not with the other gardeners?"

"Yup," Philip nodded. "Mr. Hastings took me in as I told you. I hope that doesn't turn you off, seeing as though I live in a mansion. Especially now that Madam Lafon has changed your mind about that sort of thing."

Pearl laughed. "What would turn me off is if you pretend you own it. You should save money and have contingency plans, just in case Chex kicks you out one day."

"He wouldn't," Phillip chuckled. "Half the time, Chex doesn't know that I am there. The place is so big we don't get in each other's way. He has his own space. I have mine. We don't have to meet if we don't want to."

"I was kicked out of a place I thought was my own space," Pearl sighed, "but alas, it was not mine. It was owned by my stepbrother Leonard. He built it for me, but it was only mine once I played by his rules. All I am saying is things can change. I wouldn't be so certain about what the future holds."

Phillip nodded. "That's true. Tell me about you and Leonard."

"This is not a first date conversation," Pearl said.

"So you slept with him. He was your lover," Phillip stated.

Pearl groaned. "I don't want to talk about it."

"I am not a prude," Phillip said. "I know you have lived life. So have I."

"Yes, he was my lover," Pearl said. "I don't like talking about it because it was transactional. The truth is, I was little more than a prostitute. He built me a house; I lived in it with my daughter. He sent me to driving lessons, paid for me to finish my high school subjects, and paid for me to do business management at a vocational training school.

"In return, I had sex with him about once a week. I went to his house on the hill and dressed in whatever he told me to wear. We had sex. I acted as if I enjoyed it and then that he was the best man in the world. After that, I went home and showered at least five times. That continued for years. No matter how hard I tried, I couldn't rid myself of the dirty feeling."

"Oh, Pearl," Phillip whispered.

"I got a break from him when I hit thirty. He doesn't mess with women over thirty."

"Yikes," Phillip whistled. "How old is he?"

"Fifty-six," Pearl grimaced. "You really destroyed the effect of the rose tea with talk of Leonard."

"Sorry," Phillip said. "You may have felt like a prostitute, but you weren't. What you describe is what a lot of people call relationships."

"I know, but I couldn't get over the transactional part of it," Pearl sighed. "I didn't feel anything when I was with him. I neither loved him nor hated him. I was indifferent. Numb. I learned to detach myself from the whole thing. That's how some prostitutes do it, you know. They either use drugs to cope, or they compartmentalize like I did. They reason that what they are doing is not really happening to them but to someone else."

"Some girls who danced at the club did the same thing I was doing with Leonard, with different men. I felt like a hypocrite when I was counseling them and telling them their life could be better. Everything would be different if you grew a backbone and set yourself free. Do something else with your life. You don't have to be at the whim and fancy of any man.

"And I gave them that speech while I was still in chains. You see, when you are one of Leonard's women, you are his exclusively. You signed up on the imaginary dotted line to forsake all others. It was worse than a marriage. There could be no divorce because even if you were no longer with him, you were still his. And if you dared to look elsewhere, he would kill you. Three women dared to leave. I worked with one of them. Her name was Mandy. She was the manager when Leonard suggested I work at Sensuous City to learn the ropes. I didn't know that Mandy was being phased out and I was to be her replacement."

"Phased out?" Phillip raised his eyebrows.

"Yup, she was seeing someone secretly. Leonard knew about it but didn't say a word. It was only when Mandy decided to leave Sensuous City and marry the man she loved that I saw a side of Leonard that I didn't expect. He was livid. Enraged."

"After all the things I have done for her! She is not going to get away with this." He ranted and raved about it for days."

"I was secretly happy and supportive of Mandy," Pearl said. "I even went to her bachelorette party. She died after that party. I was so, so sad."

"How did she die?" Phillip asked.

"She mysteriously lost control of her car and ended up in a wall. We speculated that her brakes were cut. I don't know what happened, but I always knew Leonard had something to do with it."

"Oh my," Phillip whispered.

"Three women dared to leave that I know of, and all three are dead. When they leave, disaster strikes."

"Does it happen immediately?" Phillip asked.

"No," Pearl shook her head. "Funnily enough, it's when they are ready to move on. Mandy was getting married, Polly was dating a big-shot guy in the financial business and was seven months pregnant. She died after her baby shower. She supposedly drowned. Dania was preparing to leave for the US. She had packed up her house, the house Leonard bought for her, moved in with a relative, and was throwing a big farewell party when she had a sudden heart attack that night."

"How old was she?" Phillip asked.

"Twenty-eight," Pearl whispered. "She never had a heart condition before."

"Are you sure they weren't coincidences?" Phillip asked.

"Very sure," Pearl said. "Leonard liked to point out how 'bad' things happened to the women who left him. It seems as if leaving me has the side effect of death. He would joke."

"I see," Phillip narrowed his eyes. "What's this guy's name again?"

"Leonard Crooks," Pearl sighed. "I planned my escape for years. I only stayed in it because I had Jewel. So I left when she was settled. I didn't even get to be at her housewarming party."

"Because basically, you are living like a fugitive," Phillip said. "This guy needs to be stopped."

Pearl laughed drily. "Phillip, I didn't tell you any of this for you to do anything about it."

"I know," Phillip said. "But for some strange reason, I am compelled to live up to my name."

"Like a knight in shining armor from a long time ago, just in time, you'll save the day, take me to your castle far away," Pearl grinned. "Man, I would close my eyes and sing to that song. What was the name of it again?"

"Glory of Love," Phillip said. "Isn't it ironic? I am a Knight and will save you, Miss Day."

"It's a nice thought, Phil, but Leonard is too rich, connected, and mean to be fought. I have resigned myself that he will get me one day," Pearl sighed. "He always gets the women who leave somehow. I won't see it coming. I am just happy that Jewel is settled and happy and doesn't need me anymore."

"I don't like it when you talk like that," Phillip said. "You talk like that because you haven't had anyone to fight for you. I'll do it. I'll be the hero you are dreaming of. And then we'll live together, knowing that we did it all for the glory of love."

"As I said, I love that song," Pearl giggled. "Why are you still single? You are handsome, well-read, charming, make the nicest rose tea, and are a great listener. I keep finding myself telling you stuff I shouldn't."

"I am happy you can be honest with me," Phillip took her hand and kissed her fingers.

Pearl felt a fissure of electricity travel all the way up her arms.

She was happy when he released her hand.

"Well, I am just recently single I was in a relationship until a few months ago. We were together for six years. It was long distance. She wanted to keep things the way they were. I wanted more."

"I see," Pearl said. Rubbing her hand, it still tingled.

"What about you? Why are you still single? You escaped Leonard, and you ran with Chex's crowd. I thought one of the guys would have convinced you to go for him already."

Pearl smirked, "I haven't really liked men. I mean, like genuinely like them. Don't get me wrong, I don't think I am gay, but I find men very resistible."

"You were basically in an abusive relationship for years. That's understandable. You have never been loved before, Pearl. Every person deserves to have that at least once."

Pearl swallowed. "That's so true. I was like a concubine in a harem. I existed to please the king, and if I wanted a normal life, I couldn't leave. My fate, if I left, was certain death. Who knew that I, a twenty-first-century woman, could relate to one of those stories?"

"That's not even funny." Phillip winced.

"I know, but it is what it is," Pearl nodded. I think I have resigned myself to the fact that there will probably not be anyone for me. You are the first...

"The first what?" Philip asked huskily.

"The first man that has ever made me think twice," Pearl said, "What I feel for you is kind of scary. It's the unknown."

"You know I feel the same way about you," Philip said. "I think we have the potential to have something unique."

"But I'm taking things slow," Pearl said. "I'm not rushing headlong into anything. So if you think that fancy French food and rose tea will change a lifetime of biases against the male of the species, you are wrong. I have never been courted before; I have never been treated like I am a being with a brain. I would like that, please."

Philip intertwined his fingers with hers and squeezed. "I can respect that. I want to give you something you have never had."

Pearl smiled and leaned her head on his shoulder. "Thank you, Philip. It means a lot to me."

They sat there for a while, silently enjoying each other's company. For the first time in a long time, Pearl felt truly content.

Chapter Eight

Phillip couldn't wait until Pearl left to make some calls. He had enjoyed their time together but this was urgent. His first call was to the head of the company that provided security for all of his companies. If anybody knew what to do about Leonard Crooks, it would be Saint Wiley. Wiley Securities were the best in the business.

"Hey, Phillip," Saint said. He was unperturbed that Phillip was calling him at that hour. It was a little after ten, but Phillip couldn't wait. He knew Saint was thorough and worked quickly.

He had been calm around Pearl, but he was really feeling livid. How dare that man threaten her life like that?

"I need to know everything there is to know about Leonard Crooks from Trelawny. And I want to take him down."

"Leonard Crooks," Saint murmured. "Okay."

"I just spoke to someone, a woman I am interested in. She is hiding out from him. She says women mysteriously die when they leave him. I want to know if he can be tied to their deaths. And I want her to be free, so I need that man neutralized by whatever means necessary."

"I am on it," Saint said. "I have heard that name before… Leonard Crooks. I'll let you know what I find."

"Thanks, Saint," Phillip hung up and called Chex.

"Why didn't you tell me Pearl was hiding from Leonard Crooks and fearing for her life?"

"Well, hello to you too, brother," Chex said. "I see you and Pearl are talking."

"We did talk," Phillip sighed. "I am going to do something about that guy."

"If you are going after him, be careful," Chex said. "I had Danger do some checking on the streets, and he said that Leonard Crooks does not get his hands dirty, which means you won't be fighting him; you'd be fighting somebody he hires. It could be someone really awful."

"I figured as much," Phillip murmured. "That's why I am hiring Saint Wiley to do this."

"Are you sure you want to do all this for Pearl?" Chex asked.

"I am sure. I think she is worth fighting for," Phillip said. "From the moment our eyes met in the garden, I have felt a connection."

"How does that feel?" Chex asked, with genuine curiosity.

"I can't describe it with words, Chex. Being around her feels right, like we were meant to be together. I know it might sound cliché, but that's how it feels. And I'm willing to do whatever it takes to be with her. And for the moment, that involves keeping her alive."

"Let me know if I can help," Chex said. "I like Pearl."

When Phillip hung up the phone, he felt like heading to Trelawny and confronting Leonard himself. But that wouldn't be smart. He went for his work laptop. He decided to catch up on his emails because he was on vacation didn't mean that his attention was not needed for some things. The first note was from his secretary.

"Gentle Reminder, Sir, Edwin Pitt's retirement party is in four weeks. You are going to do the main speech. Since this falls within your vacation time, do you want someone else to do it?"

"No," Phillip wrote back. "I will make the time to see off Edwin."

He had to do the speech. Edwin had been a manager at the first Hastings Hardware store from his grandfather's days. And he had faithfully served the company for years. He was well past retirement age, but he had asked Phillip to stay on so that he could be spared from going home to doing nothing. Phillip had agreed, but now Edwin was finally ready to retire, and Phillip had to show up to see him off.

He hoped the Leonard issue would be resolved by then. He would tell Pearl who he was, and they could go together. He was looking forward to that.

****

Natalia was dubbing it the 'great' courtship. When Pearl arrived at the office every morning, a rose was on her desk with a note. After their first date, where she had told him about her Leonard issue, she had half expected him to think that her situation was too problematic and find excuses to avoid her.

Instead, she had found a single orange rose on her desk and, with it, a note. Pearl is like the orange rose. She stands out in a sea of flowers. Her vibrant color and gentle grace, leaves me mesmerized for hours. Thank you for the first date. What about a second?

Yes, please, she smiled widely. This man was definitely different. Maybe he was like a knight in shining armor from long ago. She didn't even have to ask Natalia what orange roses meant. Natalia informed her readily.

"Orange means desire and fascination. He is saying he is fascinated with you. And a single orange rose makes a statement. Good Lord, I want to be courted by a gardener. I am telling Nathan to change his job."

Pearl laughed. "What does Nathan do?"

"IT consultant at a hotel." Natalie said, "not a very romantic job at all."

Pearl laughed. "I don't think it's the job. It's the man. Phil is unique. How many gardeners do you know who write poetry and send flowers?"

How many gardeners would listen to her deep dark secrets and the loathing she felt for herself and still want to date her.

He probably didn't understand the seriousness of what she was telling him about Leonard. He had commented that he would be her knight in shining armor, but it was all just talk. What could her little gardener do?

****

Two weeks later, she opened her door to a rapid knock. Pearl glanced at the clock; it was a little after five. Phil was standing at her door. They had been seeing each other every night of the week. Last night they had played Scrabble and chatted until late. She probably fell asleep after one.

But there he was, standing at her door with a smile. "Want to go for a swim?"

"I feel like I just fell asleep," Pearl groaned. "The water is probably cold now."

"Let's find out," Phillip grinned. "It's invigorating at this time of day. I read somewhere that there is a correlation between swimming in the morning and your productivity for the day."

"Okay," Pearl said. "Let's test that theory."

"So, did you sleep well last night?" Phillip asked when they were walking down the steps toward the beach.

"Well enough," Pearl said. "I can't understand why you have to question me repeatedly about Leonard. Since I told you about him, you've been relentless."

"I ask you about other things," Phillip chuckled. "I now know that your favorite color is… purple, all shades. It doesn't matter."

"Yes," Pearl chuckled. "Jewel couldn't stand it. She said when she had her own home, she would never put purple in it. I spoiled it for her. She has her own place, but I haven't gotten the chance to see it."

"You miss her, don't you?" Phillip asked.

"Of course," Pearl said. "For years, it was just us. She's more than a daughter; she's a friend. My very close friend, who I would protect with my life."

Phillip smiled. "I like you like this."

"Like what?" Pearl asked.

"Mother hen mode," Phillip smiled. "I want to talk to you about something."

"What?" Pearl turned to him when they touched the sand. The sun was just beginning to come out. The sea was not exactly calm, and it didn't look inviting.

"I called a friend of mine, he owns a security company, and I asked him to check out Leonard Crooks."

"You did?" Pearl breathed. "And?"

"The guy is clean as a whistle," Phillip inhaled. "If he did anything wrong, he knows how to distance himself from it."

Pearl's shoulders slumped. "I know. I can't prove anything. It was always just a vibe I had, and the things he would say. The day before Mandy died, he came into the office and said tomorrow was a big day. A lesson will be learned. If he didn't make hints like that, I probably wouldn't have associated him with them, or if he didn't crow about a side effect of leaving him was death or that he was friends with the angel of death."

"My friend suggested a sting operation," Phillip said. "We can arrange for him to meet you somewhere, and then we either get him in a confession or attempting something."

"No," Pearl started shaking her head.

"Hear me out, Pearl," Phillip said earnestly. "You can't live like this, looking over your shoulder like you are in a witness protection program. My friend is very thorough; he has state-of-the-art equipment. We can catch him in the act of trying to harm you; we can catch him in a confession."

"It won't work," Pearl swallowed. "Of the three girls who tried to escape, none of them died by something obvious. He wasn't anywhere near them."

"You have a point," Phillip said. "The man is even more diabolical than we thought."

Pearl inhaled. "Can we forget him for a moment? It's a beautiful morning; I want to take it in."

Phillip nodded. "You are right. Let's forget Leonard Crooks for the moment."

****

By the fourth week, they were spending all their evenings together, they would hang out and watch movies or listen to music and chat.

Every night was a culinary adventure. Chef Boyne had

taken to sending them dinner because of the favor he still owed Phil, and he made it a point to offer them food from different regions. Last night they had West African cuisine, and it was so good she wanted the recipe for the jollof rice to try it for herself.

Pearl had no idea if the chef had accurate interpretations of the dishes, but she knew she was having fun.

Getting to know Phillip was exciting. She even looked forward to their morning swims. There was something about them that invigorated her for the day. She had no idea what the future had in store for her, but she knew she was living in happiness for the moment. She had an attractive man who was interested in her and was concerned about her welfare. And she would hold on to the happiness bubble until it burst. She knew it would. It always did.

She headed to the office, giving Jewel a quick call from the phone she used to call her from exclusively. She thought of it as her burner phone. Maybe she was overly cautious, but she didn't want her daughter to know many things about her whereabouts. Jewel knew she had a job; she knew she had met someone, but names and details were withheld.

"Mom," Jewel answered the phone huskily. "What time is it?"

"Eight o'clock," Pearl said brightly. "Get up, sleepyhead. Aren't you going to work today?"

"No," Jewel mumbled. "I feel as if I just came in from work."

"Ah, you did one of your late nighters," Pearl said. "Have I told you how proud I am that you are a hard-working woman?"

"You tell me every day," Jewel sounded more alert. "Guess who I ran into at the bank yesterday?"

"Who?" Pearl asked.

"Trixie," Jewel said. "She said that Leonard is not pleased with her and how she is running Sensuous City. She said to tell you that he wants you back. All will be forgiven if you just come back home."

"I am not doing that," Pearl said.

"I know," Jewel said, "it sounds like a trap."

"And I am happy right here, right now," Pearl said. "I can honestly say, for the first time since I can remember, I feel different. I love feeling this way."

"It's that guy!" Jewel giggled. "The one whose name you won't tell me. He's got you wrapped around his little finger."

"I wouldn't say that," Pearl giggled, "but it's good to love."

"So, is he rich?" Jewel asked.

"No," Pearl said.

Jewel laughed until she started coughing. "I can't believe this; my mom fell in love with a man who didn't meet her first relationship requirement. I must still be asleep. What does he do?"

"He's a gardener," Pearl said. "I don't see why you find this so funny. I told you that after speaking to your aunt Precious, I have a new perspective."

"I am still getting used to the change in perspective," Jewel said. "By the way, laughing aside, I am happy for you. I look forward to meeting him, to give him my stamp of approval."

Pearl smiled, "I have to go. I am going to enter the office now."

"Have a great day," Jewel said. "I love you, Mom."

"I love you more," Pearl said. She hung up the phone and looked at it mistily.

Chapter Nine

There was a purple rose on her desk. It was gorgeous. She picked it up and inhaled its sweet fragrance. The delicate petals felt soft to the touch, and she marveled at the beauty of the intricate patterns on its petals.

The note with it read: For you, Miss Day, from your knight in denim and cotton, to you, my dear, I vow not to be forgotten, I'll be there for you through thick and thin, with you by my side, I know we'll win.

Pearl giggled.

"Purple roses are rare!" Natalia said. "I must admit I couldn't quite believe that one was real."

"It's my favorite color," Pearl sighed. "What does it mean?"

"Enchantment and love at first sight," Natalia said wistfully. "You really have this man whipped. What are you two doing at night?"

"Natalia," Pearl chided. "We have not even kissed."

"Are you serious?" Natalia said. "What century are you guys living in?"

"This one," Pearl chuckled. "I love this. It's like a slow burn. We are getting to know each other better."

The office bell jingled, and Precious stepped in.

"So this is where you work!" Precious exclaimed when she entered the space. "I've never been to the office before."

"Come on in," Pearl smiled at her. She had not expected Precious to visit. Today was to be her last day at the villa. She hadn't seen her since the day they had lunch. Precious had booked the driver and was out and about almost every day.

"I decided," Precious sat in front of her desk and glanced at Natalia, who was pretending to be busy.

"You decided what?" Pearl asked.

"I'm going to divorce Hugo and move back to Jamaica."

"Really?" Pearl gasped.

"Yes," Precious nodded. "I am choosing happiness for the next phase of my life. I'll buy a house in Kingston, open a business, and have a baby. You have inspired me, Pearl."

"Me?" Pearl squeaked.

Philip walked into the office at the same time. He was dressed all in black, his muscles flexed under his tight spandex shirt. He was on his phone. He hung up as soon as he walked in.

"Goodness," Precious said out loud. "Who are you?"

Philip flashed white teeth in a grin in Precious's direction.

"Phil Knight, my boyfriend, love interest, and knight in denim and cotton." Pearl said frankly. Both Philip and Natalia looked at her in astonishment.

Philip recovered first and smiled. "I am what Pearl said, her boyfriend, love interest, knight in denim and cotton. And you are?"

"Precious Day, Pearl's older sister," Precious said.

Pearl released the breath she didn't know she was holding.

Precious turned to her. "He's gorgeous."

"Thank you," Pearl said. "I had nothing to do with his genetics, of course, but I accept all compliments on his behalf."

Natalia started chuckling, covering her mouth, and coughing to hide it.

"As I was saying, Pearl," Precious turned back to Pearl after looking Philip over thoroughly, "I want you to manage my store. I'll pay you twice what they're paying you here. We can get to know each other again."

Pearl cleared her throat and glanced at Philip; he and Natalia were suddenly busy.

"Umm, Precious, this is not the time for that conversation."

"I understand," Precious said, nodding. "I haven't finalized the details myself. This is just an FYI. I'll keep in touch."

She got up and walked out, giving Philip one last look over before exiting the office.

"I have to go to Kingston," Phillip said when Precious left. Her perfume still lingered in the air. "I have to personally sort out some issues with my rose shipment, among other things."

"Oh," Pearl said.

"I will be back tonight," Phillip glanced at his watch. "The driver is supposed to pick me up any minute now."

"Thank you for the rose," Pearl said. "It's pretty."

Phillip smiled. "That's a hybrid tea rose, the only bloom on the plant left. As a Knight, I had to hunt it down for you, my fair maiden."

Pearl blushed.

Once more, Natalia was pretending she wasn't listening to them with rapt attention.

"See you later," Phillip left the office.

"I don't know what you are going to do when he leaves," Natalia said in the silence. "He certainly knows how to put a smile on your face."

"Oh hush," Pearl said, she refused to think that far ahead. The west lawn was almost complete. The transformation was coming along nicely. She wouldn't panic. She would take it one day at a time.

Chapter Ten

She had no plans for tonight. Pearl felt inexplicably bereft without Phil's company. She had been spoiled by his presence every night for two weeks. She made herself a sandwich and decided to call Madge. They texted each other every day.

Madge liked to check up on her, but she hadn't heard from her in two days since Pearl told her that she was falling in love with Phillip.

Madge didn't answer the phone immediately. She was probably too busy getting ready to go to a party. Didn't she say she had a brand party tonight?

She was just about to hang up the phone when Madge came on the line.

"Pearl, I almost missed you. What's going on?"

"Nothing much," Pearl said, happy to hear her voice. "What are you up to?"

"Duke and I are fighting," Madge said. "He is going on tour for twenty-one days, I have some things scheduled for that time, and he is telling me to cancel it. Tell me, Pearl, why does he think his thing is more important than mine?"

"Well, his tour is set in stone. Planned months in advance, in coordination with several persons, you can do a workaround for your thing. You are your own boss."

"True, I just don't want him to think he is more important than me," Madge murmured, "I have to keep his ego in check sometimes, or it can get out of hand."

Pearl chuckled. "You love him. You'll work it out."

"Speaking of love, how is it going with Phil, the gardener?"

"Quite good," Pearl said. "I am just for the first-time experiencing romance. And his access to flowers makes it even more potent."

Madge giggled. "Romance is so old-fashioned."

"I am an old-fashioned kind of girl," Pearl murmured.

"Does he know you have a kid and that you are not into poor men?"

Pearl sighed. "He knows all of that. I even told him about Leonard and me."

"Is that so? Madge said, "so this is getting serious."

"It is," Pearl reclined on the settee, stared up at the ceiling fan, and watched as it went round and round.

"So, there is no hope of you returning to Sensuous City?" Madge asked.

"You know that." Pearl frowned. "Why are you asking?"

"Just checking how serious you are with this new guy and the new job."

"Quite serious." Pearl sighed. "I have never felt this way. I want this feeling to last until eternity."

"Oh wow, maybe I should come and check him out, make sure he is up to snuff," Madge said. "Besides, I miss you; some things cannot be said over the phone. I have other issues I want to talk about."

"No," Pearl said firmly, "I am not telling anyone where I am. The minute you find me, I will be exposed to Leonard. I wouldn't put it past him to spy on you to get to me."

Madge laughed dryly. "You are so right. I have to go, girly. Keep me posted."

Pearl hung up the phone. Something wasn't right with Madge. What did she need to tell her face-to-face? Was Duke cheating? When they had just gotten married, it had created quite a furor locally. Duke was a handsome, popular musician with many relationships. He had given up all the girls for an exotic dancer who looked like a barbie doll. Madge had starred as his love interest in one of his music videos, and they had taken off from there.

And to imagine, Madge had arrived at Sensuous City a couple minutes past midnight looking like something the cats dragged in. She had been nineteen years old, looking quite malnourished. She had asked for Leonard.

"He knows my mother," Madge had growled. "He'll get me a job. He owes us."

After talking gently to her and calming her down, Pearl realized that behind the defiant façade was a vulnerable girl who had gone through a lot in life. Leonard had taken over some business where her mother worked and had fired her, leaving her and the children she had destitute.

Leonard had seen Madge, spoken to her, and then ordered Pearl to hire her. "Clean her up, Pearl. Make her presentable. She looks too scrawny to be out in the front. Fatten her up and make her front table worthy."

Pearl winced. She hated when he spoke about women as if they were livestock. But what to do about it? She hadn't learned the art of standing up to Leonard quite yet. At that time, she was just the assistant manager, and Mandy was in charge.

"Are you going to help out her mother?" Pearl had asked tentatively.

"Of course." Leonard said, "I didn't realize I had fired the woman or that she even worked at the business I acquired."

Pearl had been satisfied with that response, so she had 'fattened' up Madge and paid her extra attention.

Madge always hung out with Pearl, and they became fast friends. They were ten years apart in age but had similar poverty-stricken backgrounds.

Pearl had been happy when Madge had fallen in love with Duke and vice versa. She hoped there wasn't anything too wrong happening, she felt like a heel for not telling Madge where she was staying, but she knew without a doubt that Leonard would probably have someone follow her friend.

She turned on the stereo and was settling down to read a book when she heard a knock on her door. She looked through the peephole. It was Philip. She opened the door and smiled widely. He was cleanly shaven and smelling good. She closed her eyes and inhaled.

"You smell good."

"So do you," Philip held up a bottle of wine. "Home-made rose petal wine, straight from my kitchen. It's the weekend. I thought we'd celebrate, girlfriend."

Pearl groaned. "I'm sorry about claiming you so aggressively earlier. I didn't like how my sister was looking at you today. And I got inexplicably jealous. "

"No need to apologize," Philip stepped inside. "I liked how you claimed me. It made refusing her when she followed me to the west lawn even more satisfying."

"She followed you?" Pearl murmured. "Even though I told her you were my boyfriend?

"Oh yes, she followed me, told me she was interested in me, and that I should come back to the villa with her, blah blah," Philip sat beside her. "I hope you don't consider working for her. She is your sister, and all but goodness, she is something else."

"I won't even think of it," Pearl said. "I like my job here. And I have recently discovered something about myself, my decisions are not driven by money. I stayed with Leonard because of my daughter. When she didn't need me to back her financially anymore, I left."

Phillip reached across and kissed her on the lips. "You are a good person."

Pearl smiled.

"What are you reading?" Philip sat beside her.

"Some book I had packed when I was leaving Cascade Hills. I wasn't really concentrating at that the time, I just threw it in my bag. I am so happy I didn't leave it behind." Pearl said.

Philip picked up her book and looked at the title. "The Meaning of Worth."

"I had bought it for one of my girls at Sensuous City. She left before I could give it to her. I have been reading it on and off for weeks."

"And what does it say?" Philip murmured.

"Your worth is not determined by external factors such as material possessions or societal status but rather by your intrinsic value as a human being. It encourages the reader to embrace their true self and prioritize personal growth and fulfillment over external validation."

"That's heavy stuff." Phillip nodded, "and so true. Tell you what, I'll find the audiobook. We'll both listen to the book, sip some wine and have a night of it."

"So this is what dating is like?" Pearl handed him a glass of wine.

Philip nodded. "I like this. Just two people listening to a

book, drinking wine made of rose, of course."

Pearl grinned. "You really have an obsession for roses."

"And a Pearl obsession. You've gotten under my skin, taken hold of me, with a tight grip," Philip said. "Did you know that pearls are rarer than diamonds?

He drew her close and then leaned in and kissed her without hesitation. Pearl was taken aback by the sudden physical contact and felt a shock run through her body, causing her knees to weaken.

The rush of overwhelming sensuality hit her like a wave, as she had never been less prepared for anything in her life. She was enveloped in the exotic scent of his cologne, and his body's strong, muscular build pressed against her soft curves while his mouth demanded her attention.

Even though a voice in her head screamed for her to resist and pull back, her body sang a different tune, craving more of him. She felt wild and yearned for much more, a first for her on any physical level with a man.

"This wine tastes so good from your lips," Philip breathed in a roughened undertone.

"We've only known each other for four weeks," Pearl said breathlessly.

"It feels like longer," Philip said.

"So where are we going with this?" Pearl asked.

"Marriage, family, forever together if you'll have me," Philip said. "We're not getting any younger, and we both want the same thing. If you want us to wait until our honeymoon, you're going to have to stop clinging to me like this, Pearl."

Pearl moved even closer. "I think I'm throwing caution to the wind."

"No, you are not," Phillip eased away from her. "Remember, you told me that you want to experience things the traditional way. You had never been courted before, never had a man properly respect you as a human being with a brain. I am willing to give you that experience. You'll have to give me some space, though. The very scent of you is driving me wild. I don't know how much more of this I can take, but I am willing to try if you are."

Pearl was pondering why she had said all of that to him. She wanted to jump him so bad. She wanted to destroy whatever rules she had laid down. She hadn't felt like this before. She didn't care about tradition. What had she been thinking? But she wasn't a teenager anymore. She was an adult woman, and yes, her dormant sexual urges had suddenly risen to the fore, but if she wanted the full experience, she would have to be patient and allow things to progress at a slower pace.

As much as her body yearned for him, she knew that rushing into things could lead to regrets.

She took a deep breath and pulled back slightly, trying to regain her composure. "You're right," she said, her voice betraying a hint of disappointment. "I guess I just got carried away in the moment."

Philip smiled reassuringly at her. "It's okay," he said. "We have plenty of time to explore our feelings for each other. And who knows, maybe the anticipation will make it even better when we finally become intimate."

Pearl felt a sense of relief wash over her. He was right. Waiting and taking things slow was the right thing to do.

She smiled back at him, feeling grateful for his understanding and patience. "You're a good man, Philip," she said. "I'm lucky to have met you."

Phillip's eyes softened as he gazed into hers. "I want to be the man who supports you, challenges you, and loves you for who you truly are," he said, his voice low and sincere. "I don't want any doubt about the feelings part of things."

Pearl felt her heart swell with warmth at his words. Maybe this was what she had been missing - not just physical pleasure, but a connection that went beyond the surface level. And maybe, just maybe, Phillip was the one who could give that to her.

"Before I forget," Phillip murmured in her hair, "Saint wants to meet with you tomorrow. He'll be here around midday."

"Who is Saint?" Pearl murmured.

"My security company friend I was telling you about." Phillip said, "he has an idea. I think it is a good one."

Chapter Eleven

A single red rose was at her doorstep when Pearl woke up the next day. She didn't have to ask what red roses meant. There was also a note with it.

I wanted to write an elaborate poem, but I simply want to say I love you. A single red rose symbolizes the giving of your heart. I know you've been following up on the rose colors and their meaning.

Pearl felt weak in the knees, and she leaned on the door.

Her heart swelled with emotion as she read Phillip's note. She hoped he felt the same way about her, but seeing the single red rose and reading his heartfelt words confirmed it. She couldn't wait to see Phillip and thank him for the beautiful gesture. She spent the morning in a daze, feeling like she was walking on air. She couldn't stop thinking about him and their future together.

She went over to his cottage near midday. He was there with Saint Wiley.

She didn't get to say anything to him personally except a smile and an acknowledgment that she got the rose and the note.

Saint Wiley was all business; he had collected so much information on Leonard it was mindboggling.

"Leonard Crooks has twelve businesses: two motels, two restaurants, two laundromats, two mini-marts, one car mart, a pest control and chemical processing plant, and two gas stations. His real estate portfolio is extensive. He has a house in every parish in Jamaica, eight children with six different women. He was married once to Fern Silver of a Crimson Hill address. She was sixty-two to his twenty-one. She died mysteriously after a year, leaving him all of her considerable assets. That's how he got his start."

"Wow," Pearl murmured. "I didn't know all of that."

"We know even the brand of toothpaste he uses," Saint said. "His regular hangouts, who he normally interacts with, basically we know quite a bit about the man."

They were sitting in Phillip's cottage at the dining room table. Pearl kept looking between him and Saint in a daze. Saint was impossibly good-looking. The guy had green eyes and caramel skin. He looked like a painting with his chiseled jaw and solemn expression.

"My team and I have worked out precisely how we think he murdered those women."

"Really?" Pearl sat up straighter. "So it's true then, not just speculation on my part?"

"We think so," Saint nodded. "After analyzing his companies, we have concluded that eighty percent of his workforce are women. They run his businesses. He has all women lawyers and accountants. Every one of them has some ties to him in some way. He either sent them to school, gave them loans, had relationships with them, bought them houses, or paid their mortgages. He became indispensable to them."

Pearl winced. "That is his MO."

"It is a type of indentured servitude," Saint said, "where he pays for things in order to bond them to him. Except in the seventeenth and eighteenth centuries, when that type of thing was popular, there was a time limit for the servant. In Leonard's system, there is no time limit. He is the perpetual overlord."

"I know this firsthand," Pearl muttered.

"I know," Saint said. "We did a complete profile on all the women in his employ since he acquired his pest control business from the Silver family, till now, and we concluded that he chooses the women who run his companies meticulously. They are the ones who have the closest ties to him. They owe him more than the others. Those women will do anything for him, like murder."

Pearl gasped. "Are you saying that the women who were murdered were killed by other women?"

"That's right," Saint nodded. "It checks out. Mandy was poisoned at her bachelorette party, and Polly drowned after swimming at her baby shower. There is no telling what drugs got in her system before she went swimming, and Dania had a farewell party when she had a sudden heart attack. The common denominator in all of this was a party. None of the deaths were violent crimes."

"So what are you thinking? Poison?" Phillip joined the conversation.

"That's right," Saint said. "We believe someone close to each of these women was on Leonard Crooks' payroll. Maybe they were told to spike her drinks or food. My team is leaning toward drinks. It's easier to mess with drinks."

"But who would do that?" Pearl asked, confused. "Who

would literally kill for him?"

"We examined the guest list of each of these women's parties. It wasn't easy. We had to go back six years to Mandy's party, then a year later to Polly's party, and then Dania's party."

"I was at Mandy's party," Pearl whispered. "She invited all the girls she had worked with through the years and a couple of her family members and her fiancé's family."

"We know you were there," Saint said. "And so was Madge Whitlock. She was at all three parties."

"Madge is popular with everyone. She is the kind of girl everybody relates to, and everyone loves. She's a girl's girl."

"And the only common denominator in all of this," Phillip murmured.

Pearl shook her head. "No, you are so wrong. Madge has no connection to Leonard apart from working at Sensuous City. He told me to hire her because he had fired her mother."

"She does have a connection to Leonard Crooks," Saint said. "She is his daughter. Her mother had worked for him for years while she was married to Timothy Whitlock. She was registered as his child, but the two weren't living together when Madge was conceived. In fact, Timothy was away on farm work. He had always suspected that Madge wasn't his child."

Pearl slumped in the chair. Her mouth couldn't form a word.

"Does Madge know? But of course, she does," Pearl answered for herself. "That's why she came to Sensuous City, and her own father gave her a job as a dancer."

"It seems as if they'd reached an agreement. He also takes care of her children and mother and still does, to this day," Saint said.

"Her children?" Pearl couldn't form a coherent thought.

It was one revelation after another. "Madge does not have children."

"Madge has two children, a boy, and a girl," Saint said patiently. "She gave birth when she was fifteen and seventeen years old, respectively, for Richard Spencer, a mechanic twenty years her senior who is married and lives in the same yard as she lived with her mother. He was assumed to be her uncle."

"Good Lord," Pearl murmured. "Madge has always said those children were her siblings. She is quite close to them, worrying about them, sending them things and money. They visit her regularly. The girl looks just like her. I assumed they were sisters."

"Madge has quite a few secrets," Phillip murmured.

"But a murderer can't be one of them. When I left Sensuous City, I stayed with Madge!"

"And Leonard still had hoped you would return," Phillip said gently. "You weren't interested in anyone. Madge probably reported faithfully to him that there was still the potential for you to return."

"I can't believe Madge would kill people for Leonard," Pearl said. "No way."

"There is only one way to find out," Saint said. "Throw a party. It has to be a party that indicates that you are moving on. Invite her. We'll restrict the guest list and the venue. We'll monitor her before the party to see who she interacts with. We'll see exactly where she gets her poison."

"We theorize that the kind of poison she uses has to be tasteless, colorless, odorless, water-soluble, acts relatively fast and is undetectable in an autopsy. It worked on Mandy in five hours, Polly in three, and Dania in four hours. It could be that the lethality of it depended on the amount imbibed. But whatever it is, was deadly enough to work under twenty-four hours.”

Pearl gasped. “What kind of party can we have to show her I have moved on...this is overwhelming.”

“I'll take it from here,” Phillip stood up. “Thank you for doing this, Saint.”

“Anything for you, Phil,” Saint nodded to her. “It was nice to meet you, Pearl.”

****

When Saint left the cottage, Pearl couldn't sit still. Her hands were trembling. She walked out on the patio and looked over at the pool.

She couldn’t process what she had just heard. Madge was a killer. She was in a parallel reality, where up was down and down was up.

“I still can't believe Madge killed those women for Leonard. I can't process this,” Pearl bit her lip. “I spoke to her yesterday, and she wanted to know where I was. I was so tempted to tell her too.”

Phillip hugged her. “Oh, Pearl.”

“She was probably coming over to kill me. You can't trust anyone.” Pearl buried her head in Phil's neck.

“I was hoping you could trust me,” Phillip said. “I have to come clean about something.”

Pearl raised her head and looked at him. “You are married, aren't you? I knew it! A man like you has to be married. No woman in her right mind would have just let you go because she doesn't want to get married again. I knew that story was fake.”

“Actually, it's not,” Phillip frowned. “It's real. Helena did not want to get married; we broke up. I am single, or I was until you.”

"Then what is it?" Pearl asked fearfully.

"My name is Phillip Knight Hastings, not just Phillip Knight. I stopped using the Knight when I left home at nineteen and legally changed my name to Hastings twenty-one years ago."

"Okay," Pearl said. "That's not that bad. I prefer the Knight, though. It has an old-world quality to it."

Phillip chuckled. "I am happy you are taking it well."

"How else would I take it?" Pearl asked. "I can understand a person wanting to cut ties with an abusive family like you had."

"My dad was abusive," Phillip sighed. "My mother was passive. She didn't stand up to him, except when I finished high school and graduated at the top of my class. She asked me if I wanted to stay on the farm or pursue other studies. I said pursue other studies, and she contacted her father, Eustace Hastings, and he came for me."

"Wait a minute," Pearl shook her head. "That means you are Chex's older brother."

Phillip nodded. "I am."

"He said his older brother was a former lawyer who runs the family business and doesn't know how to party and have fun."

Phillip nodded. "That's me. Except I do know how to party, I just don't particularly like it, and I have fun, except my idea of fun does not resemble Chex's."

"But you made me believe you are a gardener. I liked you as a gardener, you lied to me!"

"I never lied," Phillip said, "I just didn't tell you that Mr. Hastings was Grandpa Hastings and that I now ran his company. To be 100% honest, when Chex and I bought this property, I was a bit put out that he hired you. You didn't have any experience in running an outfit like this, and

I came here to spy on you at first to see how you would handle working here.

"At least that was what I told myself and Chex. The truth is I was shaken up by our encounter in the garden, and I wanted to get to know you better and see you every day."

"So it was easier to spy on me as a gardener?" Pearl whispered.

"I have eight weeks of vacation, and I love gardening," Phillip said, "I saw your report on the west lawn, and I thought I could tackle it myself and then spy on you in the interim."

Pearl laughed dryly. "One of my closest friends is a potential murderess, and the guy I fell in love with isn't real."

"But I am," Phillip said, "I am the same man you fell in love with, Pearl. I just happen to have a different last name and a different career. And as for your friend, I thought the best bait party would be an engagement party."

Pearl gasped. "You can't just go from, 'hey Pearl, I have been fooling you up all this time to 'let's get married.'"

"Okay," Phillip held up his hands. "I understand this will be an uphill battle, and I need to ask you properly. And you need to think about it. Is three hours, okay? We can have a twilight picnic."

"Okay, I do have a lot to think about," Pearl headed to the door. She turned back and pressed her mouth to his, kissing him passionately.

Phillip was taken aback by the sudden kiss, but he responded eagerly, wrapping his arms around Pearl and pulling her closer. They kissed for what felt like an eternity, lost in the heat of the moment.

When they finally pulled away, Phillip smiled and looked into Pearl's eyes. "I'll propose properly, I promise. And

I'll tell you everything you want to know and answer any questions you have. I don't want any secrets between us."

Pearl nodded, her heart racing. "Good," she said.

She turned and walked out the door, leaving Phillip alone in the room, his head spinning with thoughts of the future. He knew challenges would be ahead, but he was ready to face them with Pearl. Together, they could overcome anything.

Chapter Twelve

They had a picnic under the gazebo on the west lawn. It was close to sunset and as usual Phillip had arranged for Chef Boyne to cater for them.

The newly renovated gazebo glistened with fresh paint. Pearl could see the strategic placement of the flowers. Some of them were already in bloom. It was a gorgeous spot. And to top it all off, the sky was painted in orange and pink hues, and the air was filled with the sweet fragrance of the blooming flowers.

Phillip had slipped a note under her door, asking her to forgive him for not being completely honest about his name.

In the grand scheme of things, she couldn't stay mad at him about that for long. They had a sizzling attraction between them, and she loved him.

Besides, what surpassed all of Phillip's shenanigans about posing as a gardener was the fact that he was concerned enough about her to try to help her with Leonard. She was more than grateful for that.

He was not the enemy. He was the man that was saving her life. If she had continued her friendship with Madge, hers would have been an inevitable end.

Never in a million years would she have thought the enemy was a close friend.

She would have continued hiding out from Leonard with Madge, not knowing that she was seeking shelter with the actual murderess. She couldn't imagine that Madge had killed three women! Three!

The thought was scary, and she didn't want to sit alone with it. When she saw Phillip's note under the door that asked her to join him for a picnic, she was more than ready to go. Maybe it would settle her mind and make her forget the sense of betrayal and fear that was constantly trying to choke her.

He had put so much effort into this evening that Pearl couldn't help but feel touched by his thoughtfulness. They had fried chicken, potato wedges, carrot, and celery sticks with a dipping sauce that was made with sea grapes.

And to top it all off. There were chewy and irresistible brownies, just the way she liked them.

"How amused were you when I showed up in your garden with Madge and assumed you were the gardener?" Pearl asked, sipping her lemonade.

"Very amused," Phillip said, "but I liked you. It bothered me, so I took advantage of my secretary's love for watching Madge's YouTube channel and listen to her report about you."

"I never showed my face. I didn't want Leonard to know where I was. I was so cautious," Pearl sighed, "Madge must have been laughing at me. Because if Leonard had wanted me gone, she would have done it. Probably with a smile on her face too."

"She probably wasn't laughing," Phillip said, "she was probably silently willing you to go back to Sensuous City so that she wouldn't have to kill you. She seemed as if she genuinely loved hanging out with you."

"But that's how she has always been," Pearl said. "She is fun-loving and fun to be around. I imagine that is how she was with Mandy, Polly, and Dania. You have no idea how devastating this is. I can imagine how devastated Duke will be when he finds out that his wife, the woman he chose above everyone else who was bomb-rushing him, already had children who she is passing off as her brother and sister and has killed three people."

"He'll be gutted," Phillip said, "but I am sure he will be thankful that she is no longer in his life. What if one day she gets tired of him? All it would take is one drink...."

"Oh goodness," Pearl sighed, "it's crazy."

"It is," Phillip nodded. "I was thinking we could have the engagement party two weeks from now and then get married the day after that."

"Are you serious?" Pearl whispered.

"Yes," Phillip clasped her hands in his. "Pearl," he said, his voice full of emotion, "I know we haven't known each other long, but I already love you more than I can articulate. I want to spend the rest of my life with you. Will you marry me?"

Pearl looked into Phillip's eyes, feeling overwhelmed with emotion.

"Yes," she whispered. "I will marry you."

****

"The minute after Madge received your invitation, she

called Leonard," Saint said over the video conference call. "Take a listen."

"Why haven't you convinced Pearl to come back to me?" Leonard asked. "I am getting frustrated with your soft approach, Madge."

"I tried," Madge protested. "I casually mentioned that the girls would need her, that Trixie won't be able to manage the nightclub as well as she does, and she didn't listen. She was determined to escape you."

"Rubbish," Leonard sputtered. "She didn't seriously want to escape me. Pearl just wanted a break. As I reasoned, she deserves it. It is now time for her to back home."

"I don't think she will," Madge stuttered. "She uh… she uh…"

"She what?" Leonard asked impatiently. "What has Pearl gotten herself into?"

"She is getting married, and I got invited to the engagement party."

"No!" Leonard bellowed. "Pearl knows that whoever leaves me pays. She is not stupid. She knows I'll find her. She knows I can't allow her to escape me. She knows it! Who the hell is she getting married to? Is it some man that thinks he can protect her from me?"

"He's a gardener, a guy named Phil Knight."

Leonard laughed. "Now I know you are joking; Pearl is not going to date a gardener."

"She has been head over heels for him since she saw him a few months ago. I couldn't believe it myself. Apparently, they are working in the same place. She talks about him every day. Leonard? Say something."

Leonard grunted. "You need to come for the special champagne. Give it to her at the party."

"Do I have to?" Madge whined. "Can't you get somebody

else to do this? I have given enough people your special champagne now. I am tired of doing this. I don't want to anymore. Pearl is my friend; I don't want to kill her."

"If you don't do it, I will stop helping your mother and kids. I will tell your precious husband that you were a prostitute in your old neighborhood, sleeping with anyone and everyone if they offered you a box lunch. I will tell him you can't have children because of a botched abortion. I will tell him how you lied to him about your childhood and expose you to the world."

Madge sounded distressed. "Okay, I'll do it."

"Good girl," Leonard sounded pleased. "You know where to pick up the champagne. I'll call you back with the time."

"There is a special place in hell for you, Leonard. I am your daughter. I am your flesh and blood. You are using me to do your dirty deeds. I hate this!"

"But you do my dirty deeds anyway," Leonard said mercilessly. "There is a thing called free choice. You don't have to do them."

"You threaten my mother and my kids," Madge sobbed. "You threaten my relationship. You blackmail me every chance you get. You are a horrible, horrible man."

"And yet I am the man that takes care of your children, sends them to that fancy private school, bought your mother a house, and gave you a job. They will be cut off and left out in the cold if you don't toe the line. And then what?"

Madge hung up the phone.

Pearl looked at Phillip and then at Saint. "Is this enough to stop him?"

"Unfortunately, no," Saint said. "We need the champagne. We need to test its content. We will have a stronger case if we can link Leonard Crooks to the poison and find his source. Hang tight, Pearl. We'll soon get through this."

Chapter Thirteen

The stage was set. In this case, the stage was the three-bedroom suite on the ground floor of the Hastings Mansion. It was perfect for the intended showdown. It had a clear view of the pool beyond the sliding doors. It was wired for cameras, and it was the place where Pearl could pretend like she was still getting ready so that Madge could walk into the trap set up for her by Saint and his team in collaboration with the detectives who were on standby.

Pearl felt like she was literally in some kind of play, and this was not her real life. In real life, she didn't know how to act. In this staging, to catch her former friend in the act of trying to kill her, she would have to do the acting of her life.

She stared in the mirror at her reflection.

She couldn't do this. Madge would take one look at her and know that something was wrong. She was wound up tighter than a clock. She needed to think about it like a play.

Act one, she was sitting in the master bedroom in her

dress. She was supposed to be fussing with her hair when Madge came in.

Jewel would be in the room with her talking, Madge would probably find a way to be with her one-on-one, and Jewel would leave. She would find some way to give her the poisoned drink.

Except the drink wasn't poisoned. Saint Wiley and his team had exchanged the bottle the day after Madge had carried it home and had tested the contents already.

The scientist had concluded that it contained thallium, a tasteless, odorless poison that is hard to detect in the system after a person dies. It had been so potent in the champagne that one glass was enough to kill her.

They had traced it back to Leonard's pest control company, the one he had inherited from his wife. The same wife who had died mysteriously thirty-odd years ago after leaving everything to him.

Pearl inhaled shakily.

"You can do this," Phillip said, massaging her neck.

"Think about the countless other lives you will save when you get him off the streets and how all the women he has under his bondage can finally be free," Chex added. "I can barely believe any of this. I really liked Madge. Duke is going to be devastated when he hears about all of this."

"I liked her too," Jewel said, looking as scared as she felt. "But I am not really surprised about Leonard. I want him gone."

They had to clue Jewel in on what was going on. She had to attend the party so Madge wouldn't suspect anything because Pearl would not have an engagement party with her daughter there.

Pearl had not liked the idea of getting Jewel involved in any way.

"She is three minutes away," one of Saint's team members came to the door. "Places everybody. Remember, we are in the walk-in closet. The champagne is not lethal in any way. In fact, it is seltzer water. You can drink it, Pearl, and not be harmed just as we rehearsed."

Pearl nodded and inhaled.

Phillip gave her a kiss.

Chex squeezed her arm.

Jewel looked at her worriedly. "I hate that you have to see your friend like this, but I am ever so grateful that you found out what she has done because if you didn't, I would be burying you and that I cannot deal with..."

"Do not make me cry," Pearl said.

Jewel sniffed. "I won't. I am trying to get myself together. I am thinking about the end result when they arrest Madge and then Leonard. I don't know if I am in the mood to party, though."

"Me neither," Pearl sighed, "but I am thinking of it as a celebration of freedom, life, love, and finding the right man for me."

"Are you really going to marry Phillip tomorrow after all of this?" Jewel asked.

"Yes," Pearl nodded. "And then we'll have an epic honeymoon for two weeks."

"Sounds like a plan," Jewel nodded. "I was shocked out of my wits when Rory drove up here and said this is where the directions said you would be. You said he wasn't rich."

"When I met him, I thought he was Chex's gardener. I told you this before."

"I know, but this place is still shocking to take in," Jewel chuckled. "I can't believe you thought Phillip was the gardener."

"You had to see it," Pearl laughed. "He loves his plants."

"Only you would have marrying rich as your number one requirement and end up falling for the gardener only to find out he owns the gardens," Jewel grinned. "I am happy that you found love however you came to it."

"Thank you, love," Pearl smiled.

"Madge Whitlock has arrived. The security is sending her right to you," one of the men came out of the closet and then went back in.

Jewel inhaled. "Okay. You ready?"

Pearl straightened up. "Yes, I am ready."

****

"So tell me, how is it going with Bunny? Is she still acting like a pain?"

"No," Jewel swallowed. Her voice was wobbly. She cleared her throat. "Actually, Bunny is acting overly nice these days. I told her she was overcompensating, she said she had years of meanness to make up for. She is constantly sweet; I haven't gotten used to her like that yet."

"I heard you were around here." Madge pushed her head around the door. "Congratulations, bestie!"

She had the bottle of champagne in her hand.

"Thanks, Madge," Pearl hugged her former friend, feeling like a fraud.

"Duke couldn't make it," Madge said. "He had a booking for tonight and couldn't break the commitment. He sends his love, and this." She held up the champagne.

Pearl nodded. "Thank him for me."

Madge laughed brightly, maybe because she was looking for it, but Pearl realized the smile didn't reach her eyes, and her smile looked brittle. She wasn't much of an actress either. It made Pearl relax.

Madge turned to Jewel. "So Jewel, how are things?"

"Fine. Great," Jewel said. "How are you?"

"I could be better, but I am happy for Pearl, so I had to show up," Madge said. "Where's your hubby?"

"He is outside with the rest of the group. I should go and join them and leave you two to talk."

"Thank you," Madge smiled. "I haven't seen Pearl in a while. I missed her."

Jewel exited the room, and Pearl watched her fondly. "I have never regretted having her. Not for a moment."

Madge sat in the chair that Jewel vacated. "I always admired the relationship you had with each other. You worked hard for her, took care of her, and would protect her with your life, you are motherhood goals Pearl."

Pearl nodded.

"I can't believe that you are getting married, Pearl. Are you sure you want to do this? You only just met him. What's the rush?"

"I love him. I don't think it will change. I want to spend the rest of my life with him, and I don't see the point of endless months and years of courtship. I want to have more kids. I want to experience what it is like to be with someone who I genuinely feel for. I want to smell the roses with him. I just want to live."

Madge placed the bottle of champagne in the chair beside her. "We should toast to that."

Pearl frowned. "But I have no glasses in here."

"I carried my own glasses," she rummaged in her bag and withdrew one plastic wine glass. "Where's yours?" Pearl asked.

"This is it," Madge said. "I am the only one drinking tonight."

"Wait a minute," Pearl said. "What's going on, Madge?"

"The champagne is poisoned," Madge said, her eyes bright, "and I don't want to give it to you. I will not give it to you. I am tired of living like this." She popped the champagne bottle open. "Pearl, you were a good friend to me, one of the best, you were a much more decent person to me than my own mother. I have loved your advice through the years, your warmth, your love and I..." Her voice cracked.

"Wait a minute," Pearl said. "Madge, what are you talking about?"

"Leonard forced me to give Mandy, Polly, and Dania poisoned champagne. They all died because of me. I had so many secrets he used to blackmail me."

Pearl gasped. She didn't have to act out her reaction. She had heard it before, but it was all too real hearing it from Madge.

Madge poured the champagne and inhaled. "It really doesn't matter now. I told Duke all my secrets. I wrote it all down. He'll find it tonight when he gets back from performing. It's only fitting that I tell you too. I was raped continuously between the ages of thirteen to fifteen by my 'uncle,' my mother's husband's brother. You see, we had to live in the same yard as them, and the ingrate took advantage of me. All of them knew about it, including my mother, his wife, and the extended family, and no one lifted a finger to help.

"Well, my mother didn't want to talk because she depended on them for shelter and handouts. She worked in the town on weekdays and only came home for the weekends, so I was at their mercy.

"I had two children for him. When I got pregnant the third time, I was like, no way in hell, so I had an abortion. I almost died. The doctors said I might never have children again.

When I was admitted to the hospital after that episode, I refused to lie for that man again. I told a social worker what was happening, and the police got involved. He ran away, and his family shielded him until he left the country.

"After that, things got tougher for us. The family chucked us out of the yard. My mother's husband said I wasn't his child anyway. We were homeless for a while, we found lodging at whichever of my mother's family who would have us. I slept around for money and favors and then I reached a point where I didn't want to do it anymore.

"I begged my mother to tell me who my real father was so that I could at least get some help. She said she didn't want to tell me who he was because he was dangerous. She said he could be generous, but it always came with strings. And that the only reason she was free of him was that she was married to another man.

"I was desperate enough to approach him anyway. You saw my state when I showed up at Sensuous City. That man is Leonard Crooks, Pearl. And he has been blackmailing me about my past ever since."

Pearl nodded. "I know."

Madge looked puzzled. "You knew?"

"I did." Pearl nodded. "I found out recently. Don't drink the champagne. You must live to fight this. You have to testify against him. You must make him pay for his crimes."

Madge sobbed. "I have done so many bad things, Pearl. I don't deserve to live."

"Give me the glass," Pearl urged. "You deserve to live."

Madge handed her the glass. Pearl put it carefully on the dressing table and hugged her friend.

"It will be alright eventually. You are doing the right thing now. You'll see."

Chapter Fourteen

After the night she had, Pearl didn't know if she would wake up for a ten o'clock wedding, but she had woken up. Jewel and Rory were staying at the guest suite with her, and they were in the living room watching the news.

"The news broke!" Jewel said excitedly. "They got him at home. Look at him. He's so pathetic!"

Pearl looked at the screen, where there was a picture of Leonard handcuffed and led to a police car.

"Local businessman Leonard Crooks is being charged with several crimes today," the news person announced. "Murder, blackmail, conspiracy to commit a crime. His reluctant accomplice, YouTube star Madge Whitlock, and wife to DJ Duke turned herself in to the police last night and gave a full confession of all the crimes committed by Crooks and herself. The police also confirm that they have airtight evidence of the crimes."

"In the meantime, DJ Duke is standing by his wife. In his

statement to the press," he said, "It will all work out in the end. I will always love Madge."

"Aw," Jewel looked at her mother, "You okay?"

"Not really," Pearl said. "I cried like a baby last night when they took her away. It's yet to be seen how many years she'll get. And how this will play out. However, it does. I am sticking by her. She would have rather died than kill me, and I'll always remember that."

"Yes, I knew you would. Loyalty begets loyalty," Jewel nodded. "I am super grateful to Phillip for making this possible. I hope they don't drag this out in court for too long. I want Leonard locked up and out of the way for a long time."

"I second that," Rory said. "Now you are free, Pearl."

"I am," Pearl inhaled. "And I can't wait to marry my knight in shining armor."

****

The wedding was a small affair in Phillip's Garden. The place where they had first seen each other mere months ago. It was a pretty morning, cool and cloudless. Most of the roses were blooming.

A lone violinist played the music to the song Glory of Love.

Pearl wore purple. She took the short walk to her groom, standing before the officiant with a smile on his face.

Phillip looked dapper in his tuxedo. They had agreed to write their own vows.

Pearl's vows were short and succinct. "I didn't know I would have found you; I didn't know I was looking or that I needed a knight in shining armor, a partner in all things, my best friend, and my true love. I vow to love you through thick and thin, support you in your dreams, and always cherish you."

Phillip's vows were longer but just as heartfelt. "Meeting you changed my life for the better. I admire your strength and kindness and look forward to building a future together. I promise to be there for you through all of life's ups and downs, to be your partner in every sense of the word, and to love you with all of my heart. And to borrow a line from Brian McKnight's song- Still In Love With You. When the eagles forget how to fly, When it's twenty below in July, And when violets turn red, And roses turn blue, I'll be still in love with you."

After exchanging their vows, Pearl and Phillip exchanged rings and sealed their love with a kiss. The officiant pronounced them husband and wife, and the small crowd cheered as the newlyweds walked down the aisle, hand in hand, towards their happily ever after.

The End

Discover Exclusive Offers and Be the First to Know!

If you haven't already, don't miss out on the opportunity to join my New Release Newsletter! Sign up today and become part of an exclusive community where you'll be among the first to hear about my latest book releases and take advantage of special prices.

Why join my mailing list?

ଓBe the First: Get a head start and be the first to know when I release a new book.

ଓExclusive Discounts: Unlock special prices available only to subscribers. Enjoy limited time offers and save big on your favorite books.

ଓQuick and Easy: Signing up takes less than 30 seconds.

To join, visit https://www.brenalbar.com/newsletter or scan the QR code below.

Thank you for your support, and happy reading!

The Crimson Hill Series

Where family drama, romance, and a touch of sci-fi blend seamlessly in the enchanting backdrop of a small town in Jamaica. Prepare to embark on an unforgettable journey as secrets unravel, passions ignite, and destinies intertwine.

No Goodbye (Book 1)
No Misunderstanding (Book 2)
No Ordinary Love (Book 3)
No Fairy Tale (Book 4)
No Letting Go (Book 5)
No Strings Attached (Book 6)
No More Mrs. Nice Girl (Book 7)
No Place Like You (Book 8)
Knight and Day (Book 8.5)
No Expectations (Book 9)
Ice and Fyre (Book 9.5)
No Surrender (Book 10)
No Time for Love (Book 11)
No Promises (Book 12)
Winter's Eve (Book 13)

The Wiley Brothers

Step into the world of the Wiley Brothers, where tragedy weaves an unbreakable bond and love becomes their guiding light. In this captivating series, follow the journey of six remarkable boys as they navigate the tumultuous path of growing up without parents, discovering love, and finding their place in a challenging world.

Between Brothers (Book 0)- How it all began…
For Pete's Sake (Book 1)- Preston's story.
Crossing Jordan (Book 2)-Jordan's story.
Fire and Walter (Book 3)- Walter's story.
The Perfect Guy (Book 4)-Guy's Story.
The Patience of a Saint (Book 5)- Saint's Story.
A Case of Love (Book 6)- Case's Story.

The Pryce Sisters

Follow the remarkable journey of the Pryce triplets as they navigate the complexities of growing up, discovering romance, and embracing the exhilarating challenges of the new adult years.

Baby For A Pryce- Book 1
Right Pryce Wrong Time – Book 2
Yours, For A Pryce- Book 3

The Jacksons

Prepare to be enthralled by the captivating saga of the Jackson family. In this gripping series, secrets unravel, paternity questions loom, and love blooms in the most unexpected corners.

Ace- Book 1
Deuce- Book 2
Trey- Book 3
Quade- Book 4

The Scarlett Series

Their patriarch died and unexpectedly left each of them a fortune. Watch as the Scarlett family navigate their way through the ups and downs of sudden wealth, family secrets, and the complicated dynamics of their relationships.

Scarlett Baby (Book 1)
Scarlett Sinner (Book 2)
Scarlett Secret (Book 3)
Scarlett Love (Book 4)
Scarlett Promise (Book 5)
Scarlett Bride (Book 6)
Scarlett Heart (Book 7)

Magnolia Sisters

They were the rejects. The worst of the lot, they grew up in a girl's home together and formed sisterly bonds. Each book in the series tells the story of a different girl and the unique struggles and triumphs she faces along the way. With themes of friendship, forgiveness, and the power of love, the "Magnolia Sisters" series is a heartwarming and inspiring read that you won't want to put down.

Dear Mystery Guy- Book 1
Bad Girl Blues- Book 2
Her Mistaken Dream- Book 3
Just Like Yesterday – Book 4

New Song Series

A group of friends started out as a church band, see how each of them navigate their personal and professional lives while staying true to their faith and facing challenges along the way. With themes of forgiveness, redemption, and second chances, the New Song Series is a captivating read for anyone who enjoys heartwarming stories of love and faith.

Going Solo- Book 1
Duet on Fire- Book 2
Tangled Chords- Book 3
Broken Harmony- Book 4
A Past Refrain- Book 5
Perfect Melody- Book 6

The Bancrofts

The Bancroft family delves into the inner workings of academia and the high-stakes world of university politics. The family wrestles with the pressures of maintaining their family's legacy, they must confront their own demons and navigate the complex relationships that bind them together. From unexpected love affairs and betrayals to scandals and secrets that threaten to tear them apart, this is a series that will keep you captivated until the very end.

Homely Girl- Book 0
Saving Face- Book 1
Tattered Tiara- Book 2
Private Dancer- Book 3
Goodbye Lonely- Book 4
Practice Run- Book 5
Sense of Rumor- Book 6
A Younger Man- Book 7
Just To See Her- Book 8

Three Rivers Series

Three Rivers Series, a captivating tale of love, redemption, and second chances set in a picturesque community in St. Ann's Bay, Jamaica.

Private Sins- Book 1
Loving Mr. Wright- Book 2
Unholy Matrimony- Book 3
If It Ain't Broke- Book 4

The Resetter Series

The Resetter Series takes a look at a rare kind of person, a person who can travel back in time, but they only have one chance to get things right if they go back! With themes of second chances, changing the past and the power of love, the resetters series is a captivating time travel romance that many readers have described as a page turner.

Never Too Late- Book 1
Never Say Never- Book 2
Now or Never- Book 3
Almost Never- Book 4

On the Rebound Series

Experience the gripping and emotionally charged On the Rebound series, where love, betrayal, and redemption collide in a whirlwind of passion and secrets. Brace yourself for a journey filled with drama, cheating scandals, DNA questions, and ultimately, the power of second chances and finding love again.

On the Rebound- Book 1
On the Rebound Book 2

Standalone Books

Full Circle- After graduating from university, Diana wanted to return to Jamaica to find her siblings. What she didn't foresee was that she would meet Robert Cassidy and that both their pasts would be intertwined, and that disturbing questions would pop up about their parentage just when they were getting close.

After the End- Torn between two lovers. Colleen married her high school sweetheart, Isaiah, hoping that they would live happily ever after, but life intruded, and Isaiah disappeared at sea. She found work with the rich and handsome Enrique Lopez as a housekeeper and realized that she couldn't keep him at arm's length.

Love Triangle: Three Sides to the Story- George, the husband. Marie, the wife, and Karen-the mistress. They all get to tell their side of the story.

New Beginnings- Inner-city girl Geneva was offered an opportunity of a lifetime when she learned that her 'real' father was a wealthy man. Her decision to live up-town meant she had to leave Froggie, her 'ghetto don,' behind. She also found herself battling with her stepmother and battling her emotions for Justin, a suave up-towner.

The Preacher and the Prostitute- Prostitution and the clergy don't mix. Tell that to ex-prostitute Maribel, who finds herself in love with the Pastor at her church. Can an ex-prostitute and a pastor have a future together?

Historical Fiction

You won't want to miss out on these two captivating reads!

"The Pull of Freedom" tells the story of a slave family and their desperate struggle for freedom in Jamaica's colonial era. Follow the journey of these brave individuals as they fight for their right to be free, facing danger, heartbreak, and unimaginable obstacles along the way.

"The Empty Hammock" takes readers on a journey through time, as a modern woman finds herself transported back to the Taino era of Jamaica's history. Experience the wonder and mystery of this ancient culture through her eyes, as she learns about their traditions, beliefs, and way of life. With richly drawn characters and a beautifully realized setting, "The Empty Hammock" is a must-read for anyone who loves historical fiction that transports them to another time and place.

Short Story Collections

Di Taxi Ride and Other Stories- Funny stories about Jamaican life to make you laugh.